BOUND TO YOU

Reed Enterprises, Book 1

M.G.

For all the mamas.

Single, married, foster, adoptive...all of you.

I see you. I feel you. I AM you.

CONTENTS

TRIGGER WARNING LIST

Stalking (not the MMC)

Mention of a Dead Animal/Animal Parts (no harm done on page)

Kink

Power Exchange

Body Shaming/Poor Self Image

Light Choking

Spanking

Bondage (mentioned)

Forced Orgasms

Light Degradation

Praise

Threats to a Child (no harm actually done)

AUTHOR'S NOTE:

Please be aware that this book is not meant to be a how-to guide in how to participate in a BDSM relationship/dynamic. Those looking to partake in any power exchange relationships/scenarios should do extensive research prior to entering into any sort of dynamic or participating in any kinks.

Knowledge is power.

Consent is key.

Boundaries are necessary.

CHAPTER 1

Hope

I shouldn't even be out right now, not with the interview lined up for Monday morning.

The noise in the bar is ridiculous.

Okay, it's probably normal for a weekend, but I had planned to be in my comfy clothes with a book and a glass of wine right about now. Why did I agree to come out again? I'm so damn uncomfortable in these jeans. They're from last year so they're a little more snug than what I'm comfortable with. It's harder to lose the baby weight than I thought. Ginny and Katy twisted my arm and even went so far as texting my parents to watch the rugrat so they could drag me out kicking and screaming, and they're not even here yet!

Rude.

Whatever. At least I can sit in my little corner and people watch until they get here. I love people watching and creating little made-up stories about their lives. Like the twenty-something year old woman in the mini-skirt at the other end of the bar twirling her hair and looking bored. In my head, she's meeting some blind date. She didn't want to come out, but her grandmother set her up with someone from the local church without telling her and she would hate to upset the woman. I imagine the "nice young man" she's been set up with is actually someone a bit older than she would normally go for. Maybe he's surprisingly good looking, but utterly dull in the conversation department.

I giggle into my drink and continue my perusal. There are people milling about at high-top tables talking while the more drunken patrons dance around the small open space available in front of the stage the place uses when they have live music. The noise of the bar blurs together into a hum as I continue to look around the space, the dimmer lighting simultaneously making it easier for me to people-watch without getting busted and harder to see the people I'm trying to watch. That's when I saw him across the room and, *damn* isn't he something to look at?

Tall. At least six-foot. Thick dark brown hair that lightens as it gets farther away from the root and looks like he's spent all day running his fingers through it. From what I can tell, he has a strong jaw and a nose that looks like it's been broken in the past thanks to a little bump on the bridge. And the way he fills out that dress shirt? *Fuck. Me. Sideways.* I bet he spends a decent amount of time at the gym. Certainly more than I ever have. His biceps are big enough that you can tell he's strong, but they're not ridiculous, and his shoulders are broad and strong looking. Like he could throw me over his shoulder and walk me out of here if he wanted. *Hot.* Biting my lip, I rake my gaze lower. His chest is defined, the muscle there teasing me the longer I watch. He has a trim waist, but given how the rest of him is built, I'd bet money you'll find at least six defined abs. When he turns to the bar to order a drink, I nearly choke on mine. *Jes-us!* Don't even get me started on his ass. Adonis himself couldn't have filled out those slacks any better. *He certainly doesn't skip leg day.*

The more I look at him, the more I feel like he seems stressed. Don't ask me why that's the vibe I get, I don't know, it's just a feeling. I look back at his face and that's when I notice the lines around his blue eyes and the harshness of his clenched jaw. *Maybe that's why I get the "stressed" vibe.* You can almost see the tension he's holding back. I wonder what it is. I wonder what it would take to make those stress lines disappear.

He looks over at me and we make eye contact.

Oops. Busted.

I give a friendly smile and let my eyes scan the room, attempting to make it look like an accidental thing instead of like I was thirty seconds from having drool run down my chin.

I get lost in my head as I wait for the girls.

God only knows when the last time I had some fun for myself. I don't regret any of it. Lizzie is my life. My North Star. She's the reason I force my tired eyes open every morning with my alarm. My little girl is everything. She's all I have left of my husband. *Late* husband, I mean. Matt died just as Lizzie turned one.

What am I doing?

Staring at the man like a starstruck, lovesick teenage girl. And what sort of power does this complete stranger hold over my libido? I haven't even thought of a man in that way since Matt. And now, all of sudden, it's like my lady bits have been jolted with a defibrillator and are sitting up paying attention.

Ginny and Katy finally show up and pull me from the inner turmoil. There are greetings and hugs all around as we settle in at the bar. Out of the corner of my eye, I notice Mr. Tall and Handsome watching us and a flush of light pink crosses my face. It must be more noticeable than I thought because he smirks and winks before his gaze snags on something over my shoulder. He smiles and waves, standing up to greet another stunning man.

Hot damn! What is in their water supply and how do I get some?

His friend is even taller than him! His brown hair is

neater than Mr. Tall and Handsome, gelled in place. A cursory look tells me he's just as fit as his friend, and they both know how to command a room as every eye in the bar has turned to watch them at some point. I need to focus on my friends, not the delicious eye candy across the bar. I haven't been out in I don't know how long, and I'm here to unwind for a change. I'm always so zeroed in on Lizzie. Making sure she has everything her little heart could ever want or need. Making sure the house is cleaned as best as possible, while making sure she has my attention. I've always been the person to give all of myself to others, even when the tank is on E, I find a way to give more without taking anything in return. *Is that healthy? No. Am I going to stop doing it? Unlikely.* I don't want to be selfish, and I'm absolutely petrified to disappoint someone I love. I turn back to my friends and focus on our conversation and drinks, enjoying my night out for the first time in far too long.

As the night progresses I laugh more than I have in as long as I can remember. It's been almost three years since Matt passed, not long in the grand scheme of things, but when you combine the soul crushing grief with the stress and mental exhaustion of being a mom, it feels like it's been so much longer than it really has. Throughout the night I catch myself looking for the handsome stranger, hoping to catch another glimpse of him.

Shaking my head at myself, I realize it doesn't matter if I do or not. I can't do anything about the quickly growing salacious thoughts running through my head about a man I've never met. Even if I could, I wouldn't. I've been working part-time in a coffee shop not far from home for the last year or so and I've yet to come across a man I feel any inclination to flirt with, let alone fuck. So tonight, I need to focus on my friends and the rest of the weekend will be spent finalizing my resume and interview skills for Monday morning, making sure I perform at my best so I can provide better for Lizzie.

It doesn't matter anyway. It's not like someone like him would notice me anyway. A tired, single mom still rocking the mom pouch that won't seem to go away no matter the diet or workout plan I choose. I swear, it's damn near impossible to lose weight...

Wait...

Is he...?

Oh shit, he is.

He's coming over here!

Fuck! What do I do?! I've hardly spoken to the opposite sex in *years* outside of a workplace setting, let alone thought about flirting with the male species since before I got married. I quickly look back to the girls to see if they've noticed the absolute smoke show walking toward us— they noticed. Their eyes are wide and there are flirtatious smiles plastered on both their faces as they try to figure out who he plans to approach.

The voice at the back of my head reminds me that maybe he's just coming over for a drink. *We're in a bar, genius. Just because he's walking this way, doesn't mean he's coming to talk to you.* Sometimes, I love that voice. Obviously, he just needs a refill. I relax and go back to my friends.

I see someone sit down next to me from the corner of my eye. Chancing a glance to my right, I see it's him and I tense a little. That voice in my head tells me to calm down. His glass is empty; he clearly wants another drink and a place to sit while he waits.

Until he speaks.

To me.

In a voice Tom Hardy would be jealous of. "Is this seat taken?"

I look at my friends and then turn back to him and shake my head, too stunned to speak.

He smirks, "You mind if I join you?"

I shake my head again. Eyes wide.

He sticks out his hand to shake mine, because obviously he has manners, and says, "Hi, I'm Landon."

On reflex, I hold out my own. His hands are surprisingly calloused for someone dressed for the office. *Callouses would help explain the mountain of muscle currently next to me.*

"Hope," I reply, holding on to his hand longer than is socially acceptable. Realizing this, I quickly dropped his hand as if he had electrocuted me.

He smiles, and I swear the room gets brighter.

"Nice to meet you, Hope. What brings you out tonight?"

"Just out for a drink with my friends here. They wouldn't let me stay home."

He cocks his head to the side and looks to my friends next to me, "Why's that?"

I shrug shooting my friends a halfhearted glare and rolling my eyes, "Because it's my birthday. They told me staying home in my favorite pajamas and lounging on the couch with a bottle of wine, my favorite ice cream, and a book was sad."

He tries to hold back his laugh, but I can see it in his eyes.

"I have to say, I agree with your friends. A beautiful woman like you shouldn't be cooped up inside on her birthday. It defies nature." His eyes lazily slide over me as he continues, "No, you definitely needed a night out to celebrate."

My brain stuttered.

Did he call me beautiful?

This man. This *Adonis* of a man called *me* beautiful?

I looked over my shoulder at the girls to see if they heard the same thing as I did, because surely, he's not talking to *me*. They're pretending not to listen, but I can see the grins on their faces as they studiously sip their drinks. I'm not bad looking, but I wouldn't call myself stunning either. I'm just...*me*. Maybe he's talking to someone on an earpiece, or someone behind me that I can't see, and I've just made myself look like the biggest dumbass to ever grace the earth. At least, until my logical brain kicks in again and reminds me that he shook *my* hand and asked for *my* name.

When I look back at him, I'm blushing furiously and his brow is slightly furrowed like he's confused by my reaction. Thankfully, the girls choose that moment to step up and save me from further looking like a complete dumbass.

"Hey lovely!" Ginny says with a grin. She looks at Landon with a quick once over and asks, "Care to introduce your new friend?"

Katy, being the dear that she is, looks at me with a grin saying, "Who cares? He's cute!" Her smile turns a little devious when she asks, "What're you gonna do about it?"

Out. Loud. She said that *out. Loud!*

I sneak a peek back in Landon's direction and see him smirking into his glass. My cheeks flaming hotter than before, I look at Katy with scathing eyes that she merely shrugs at.

Landon steps in to introduce himself to them, sticking out his hand with a grin, "Landon. Sorry to interrupt your night, ladies. Hope was just about to let me buy her a drink for her birthday. Would you like anything?"

Before I could protest and tell him that's not necessary, the girls jumped in with a resounding *yes.* He just keeps grinning and shoots me a wink, causing me to choke on the gulp of whiskey I just tried to down. Ginny and Katy look at me with worried eyes and I shake my head to let them know I'm okay while everyone talks and I attempt to get air flowing back into my body.

Landon seems to actually be a nice guy. He keeps up great conversation, and actually looks you in the eye when you speak to him. I had forgotten what that was like — not just having a conversation with another adult but one that looks you in the eye. It feels like everyone is so glued to their screens, that we're losing the ability to actually speak to one another. *God! I sound old!* The girls were right to make me come out tonight. I'm having a great time and I've been so starved for social interaction I didn't even notice until now.

I need to remember to thank the girls for this.

As the drinks flow, the girls get bolder. I stopped after the drink Landon bought for us, needing a clear head to get up in the morning with Lizzie.

Katy looks at Landon with a damn near evil gleam in her eyes, and before I can stop her, asks, "So Landon, do you like kids?"

"Katy!" Ginny admonishes.

Landon chokes on his drink, coughing to clear his throat. My eyes shoot wide and I stomp on Katy's foot under the table.

I know what she's doing.

Landon glances at me with a question in his eyes before shifting his attention back to Katy.

"Can't say I've ever been asked something like that from

a stranger, but I'll play along. I love them. I'd love my own someday, but it seems that work is my only Mrs. these days, and the women I do manage to date don't stay for long."

A strange look crosses his features, something that seems to morph from sadness to resignation to something...else. I stare at him trying to decipher it and end up catching his eye. His blue eyes appear darker now. He gives me an appreciative once over, so quick I don't think I saw it correctly, but his pupils dilate, giving them a predatory gleam.

Ginny catches the look and elbows me, trying to encourage me to step into the dark promises flashing in his eyes. I give her a little pinch in answer.

She and Katy look at each other, a silent conversation passing.

What are they plotting?

Ginny looks back at me and announces that she and Katy are going to go dance, knowing good and well I haven't had enough to drink to get up myself. They head out, leaving me and Landon at the table. Alone.

Traitors.

Landon looks at me with a smile and asks, "Care to enlighten me?"

I act as nonchalant as I can and return, "About what?"

He simply smiles wider. Little dimples forming next to his perfectly plump and kissable lips, I want to see more of it. "We can start with why a perfect stranger just asked me what I thought about kids, and we can work our way around to why you stomped on Katy's foot and pinched Ginny."

"Ah, caught that did you?"

"I did."

I sigh. Might as well tell him. *His attention was nice while it lasted.*

"I have a daughter. And my friends are under the impression you're attracted to me and are trying to force my hand in admitting it's mutual...which I guess they did..." my cheeks are burning as I continue while looking at the table. "They seem to think that I need to get back on the horse and start dating again."

I look back up at Landon after a long beat of silence. His eyes are blazing.

He takes me by surprise when he gruffly asks, "You're attracted to me?"

Okay, not what I thought he would choose to focus on...

Blushing— *why do I keep blushing?!*— I nod. Too dazed and confused to verbalize my response. *He does own a mirror, right?*

"And you haven't dated in a while? Why is that?"

Shit. I do *not* want to get into this. Emotional trauma dumping is not something you get into with a sexy stranger.

I look away when I reply, "I'd rather not talk about it."

He doesn't seem to like that response, but he doesn't push. Thankfully. He comes back around to the thing that will finally send him running.

"What's your daughter's name?"

"Lizzie."

"How old is Lizzie?"

"She's turning three soon," I reply with a dreamy smile.

Landon further surprises me when his whole face lights up. "I love that age! They're so inquisitive and trying to figure out the world. Always pushing boundaries, it seems."

What. The. Fuck?

He actually likes kids? He wasn't just saying that earlier? This is *not* how I saw this conversation going. While I'm lost spinning in my head, Landon is looking at me with questioning eyes. I wonder what he's thinking about. To turn the conversation I ask, "What's that look?"

He pauses, appraising me, "Can I ask you something?"

Confused and feeling a little flirty now that I know he's not going to make some shitty excuse and bolt, I return, "Isn't that what you've been doing?"

He laughs. "Yes, but this is something else. Something personal."

And what he's been asking isn't personal?!

I'm both petrified and curious about the question running through his mind.

Fuck it. We've come this far.

I shrug, "Sure. Might as well."

"Keep in mind, you can tell me to fuck right off and leave you alone...although I would prefer you just not answer the question. I'd very much like to continue talking to you."

Now I'm confused. What the hell could he possibly want to ask?

Looking me dead in the eye, Landon asks me the LAST thing I expect.

"Are you familiar with kink? Specifically, the roles of a

Dominant and submissive?"

Huh.

CHAPTER 2
Landon

She's perfect. Curvy little thing. She can't be taller than 5'6. Long hair, just enough to hold in my fist. I can't figure out the color…is it red? Brown? Something in between? Maybe burnt copper? Like when it hasn't been polished in a while. She's trying to hide in her clothes, but I see her. The way she fills out the jeans she's wearing with thighs thick enough to swallow me whole. The curve along her ribs and above her hips tells me she's not afraid of food, *I love a woman I can share a real meal with.* She's somewhere between an hourglass and pear-shaped. Her breasts seem to be enough to overflow from my hands, but not so big I'd drown if I ever got the chance to suck them.

Physically, she's everything I've been looking for in a woman. I'm definitely attracted to her…

That's it! No more staring. I *have* to know her. Everything about her.

Her eyes are what draw me in. The lightness of them. So blue, they're silver— glacial. The lines around them tell me she likes to smile and laugh, and that she does it often. But the darkness underneath? She's tired. What could it be that's putting them there? What is it keeping her up at night? If she were mine, the answer to that question would be me.

Fuck it. I'm going to talk to her.

I give James some half-assed excuse and walk away, my eyes never leaving her. I vaguely hear him laughing as I make my way to her. As I approach, I can see the eyes of several men throughout the bar watching her and her friends. All three women are beautiful, but I only have eyes for *her*.

I need to know if she smells as sweet as she looks. I want to know what makes her smile so much to put those lines by her eyes. I have this inexplicable need to solve whatever issue is keeping her up at night...or add to it; depends on if fucking her all night is a bad thing or not.

My mind continues to wander as I make my way over to her...I need her taste on my tongue as she drips down her thigh. I want to see the way the muscles in her legs tense when she comes.

Stop it, Landon. Focus.

***

Our conversation is easy, fluid.

I can't remember the last time I had such a free flowing and pleasant conversation with a woman. Most of the time they're just looking to hook up or they notice the expensive suit and watch. I slowly inch my way closer to Hope throughout the night. I don't think she's noticed and I can't seem to help myself. The space between us feels magnetized.

Then we're left alone when her friends get up to dance.

Perfect.

***

I definitely didn't see myself asking her *that*. For fuck's sake, she doesn't need this kind of shit. A single mom to an almost three-year-old little girl. She shouldn't be looking at me right now with curiosity in her eyes. She should be out on the dance floor with her friends, carrying on and having a good time.

Instead, she's still in this booth with me. Nibbling on her lower lip as she contemplates her answer.

I *need* her to answer my question.

I'm on pins and needles, anxious that I've pushed too far. I would understand completely if she got up and all but ran away from me. *I certainly wouldn't blame her.* I mean, honestly,, who the fuck asks a complete stranger if they're familiar with kink?!

I'm about to apologize, ask her to forget about it, and beg her to stay and keep talking to me, but she beats me to it and shocks the hell out of me when she doesn't start cussing me out.

"Maybe?"

Huh? Maybe what? Oh! Right. I asked her a question.

She poses her response as more of a question than an answer. She seems hesitant, and I suppose that's fair. It's not like this is something I have any right to an answer to.

"Where have you heard about it? If you don't mind my prying."

She wrinkles her nose, and damn if it isn't the cutest fucking thing I've seen all week. Her face, chest, and arms are covered in freckles and I want to spend my time kissing and counting as many as I can find.

"Umm...this is certainly an odd conversation for two strangers..."

"Okay, no worries! I'm sorry for prying. That was definitely out of line."

She doesn't look convinced. *I think I fucked up in a big way here.*

"Can I be honest?" She asks.

Shit. She's about to call me a perv and leave.

Resigned to my fate, I nod, "I'd rather you were."

She gives the briefest of pauses before muttering *'Fuck it'* to herself and takes a deep breath.

"I've always been curious about the dynamics of a relationship like that, but I don't know what all it entails and that makes me nervous to try it. I mean, I've read plenty of books that paint it in a way that's really sexy, but I've always wondered if it actually was."

I perk up. *Holy shit.*

Is this happening? Like, really happening?

"What do you want to know?" An eagerness bleeds into my voice that I hope she can't hear.

"As much as I can. I've never met anyone who openly admits to participating in kinky activities. Of course, I'm working on the assumption that you do, since you asked."

I nod again. "Yes, I'm a Daddy Dom, but I'm not 100% committed to the lifestyle—"

She interrupts me. "Pause. What's a Daddy Dom?"

"It's different for everyone. For me, I take it to mean guidance, discipline, safety, and comfort. All of these things I offer to my submissive when we enter into a dynamic."

She mulls that answer over before nodding for me to continue.

"I personally don't want anything super intense from

these dynamics, that just doesn't appeal to me. It's something I keep limited to the bedroom. I can tell you whatever you want to know, to the best of my knowledge at least, if that's something you'd be interested in."

She gestures for me to go on, seeming to be listening intently.

"Firstly, when I say I'm not in the life 100%, I mean I'm just someone who enjoys aspects of it, not one that lives it full-time. Secondly, it's all consensual from both parties. Sex isn't always a part of Dominant/submissive relationships. There are always strong boundaries set by both parties that must be adhered to for the relationship to work, whether or not sex is involved. Like I said before though, I'm not a person interested in a full immersion into a dynamic. I like taking care of my baby girl…"

I pause. I don't want her weirded out anymore than I think she already is by giving an information dump and overwhelming her, especially if she's not interested in actively engaging in this sort of thing.

However, the closer I look at her, the more it looks like her pupils are dilating as I talk. I have to remember to continue when she catches my stare, waiting for me to keep explaining.

I inch a bit closer. Our thighs now pressed together and my arm behind her along the back of the booth. My voice drops as I continue, "For myself, I like to be in control of my partner's pleasure. I say when and how she comes and how many times. When we're not in the bedroom, I want someone I can call mine. Someone to share everyday life with and someone that I can help make even the most mundane and monotonous tasks a little easier, less tedious."

She interrupts again, and I try not to switch to "Dom-mode" and correct the behavior, "Okay, I get the second part, about wanting to share your everyday life; you want a genuine relationship outside of the kink," she pauses, shifts in her seat and angles herself to face me, leans in. "Answer me this. In the books I've read, there's inevitably some sort of...punishment. Is that a part of this? I've heard of people enjoying spanking during sex, is that like, something that happens? Or is that all a massive assumption on my part?"

"There are punishments, all different kinds. Time out, orgasm denial, spanking, etcetera." I can feel my cock thickening in my slacks as her blush deepens and her pupils dilate. I can't even adjust to make myself comfortable as I continue, that's how close we are. "Punishments are only doled out based on what both parties consent to before beginning the relationship."

"Why did you ask me if I knew about this kind of thing?"

Valid.

I don't hesitate, "Because I like you. I want to take you out and date. And I'd like to talk to you about becoming my submissive at some point if that's something you'd be open to trying. It's not a deal breaker if you're not interested, so I wanted to see what, if anything, you knew and understood."

Silence. And based on her frozen expression, *stunned* silence.

Before she can outright reject me, I go on. "If you're not interested in any of what I just said, that's fine. I'd like to take you on a date regardless. Again, it's not a deal breaker for me. I don't have to have that sort of relationship to get off, it's just..."

"Wait." *Thank you, God. Did I really talk about getting off??* She has a wide-eyed expression. "Y-you want to take me on a date?"

That's what she's stuck on?

"Umm, yes. I thought I was making that obvious…"

Again, I trail off at her confused look.

"What are you so shocked about? You're a beautiful woman, and you seem kind. I've liked our conversations so far. I want more. I'd like to take you out right now if you'd let me, maybe a late-night diner? If you're feeling up to it, I could kill a couple waffles from Waffle House right about now."

"You confuse me," is all she says.

To clarify, I ask, "Me?"

She nods, "You."

"What about me has you confused?"

"Um…everything?"

"How so?"

She pauses, thinking over her answer, "My friends accost you about kids, and you don't bat an eye. You find out I have a daughter and act like it's not a big deal. And in the same breath, you both tell me you want to take me on a date and that you want me to be your submissive after explaining what that is in the first place. And you're acting so incredibly unaffected! As if you do this on a regular basis…"

Her babbling fades, and her expression is mildly incredulous. I have to chuckle.

To ease her internal struggles, "No, I don't do this regularly. I've only ever shown this side of me to a serious girlfriend. And as we established earlier, that hasn't happened in a while."

"So, what makes me so special? I'm obviously not a serious girlfriend, we just met." Her tone is bordering on indignation.

I'll let it slide for now. She's curious and has questions that need to be answered.

A small smile slides across my face without my permission, and I shake my head, "I don't know. There's something about you I feel drawn to. Something almost magnetic, I can't think of any other way to describe it…"

She nods her head in understanding, as if she feels it too. *Thank God.*

"I'll be honest with you, Hope. If we do this, I will be completely devoted to you. There won't be anyone else, for either of us. If you agree, you're mine and mine alone. I don't share, and I don't expect you to either."

I pause before I add, "And, in full disclosure, if you commit to being my baby girl later down the road, there will be punishments, and you won't like them while they're happening…" Her lustful expression douses, "…but the pleasure you'll get from the pain will be *otherworldly*, I swear."

Her eyes darken, her pupils growing in size, and her friends choose this moment to come back to the booth, panting and sweating from all the dancing. They settle in, glancing between Hope and I, who sits frozen and staring at me, and they seem to have a silent conversation with a single glance.

Misreading the tension, Katy looks at Hope and asks, "You ready to go?"

While I approve of the loyalty, it frustrates me that she thinks I've upset Hope. I would *never* intentionally upset her. In the short time we've spent talking, the connection I feel to Hope has grown to an unbelievable level; it feels like she was meant to be mine. There's just something about her that speaks to me.

I sound fucking insane, but that doesn't mean it isn't true.

Mine. The cadence plays on repeat in my head. I can't explain the instant connection, and frankly, I don't care to. I've never felt like this with anyone before, and I'm not about to let her go easily.

Ginny shakes Hope back to reality when she doesn't respond, repeating Katy's question.

Hope looks at her friends with a reassuring smile. Nodding her head, she turns back to me, and my heart sinks. Her smile shifts to a sly grin, and she gets a devious glint in her eye.

"Goodnight Landon. And thank you for the lunch invitation tomorrow."

Huh? I didn't ask her to lunch.

"Here." She holds out her phone, "I'll need your phone number so we can make plans."

Her friends look shocked, staring wide-eyed at Hope while I sit there stunned, waiting for my brain to catch up. Her face starts to fall before I can finally form a complete thought, and I jump to grab her phone. She unlocks it and hands it to me. As I plug in my number and text myself, I can't help but smile. Repeating in my mind *mine, mine, mine* over and over again.

She doesn't know it yet, but she will. I'm never letting her go now.

CHAPTER 3

Hope

"Holy shit! Did you actually say yes?!"

"I can't believe it! You said yes! You've got a date!"

The girls continue to squeal like stuck pigs in their excitement for me.

I, however, can't believe my boldness. I can't believe I *did* that. I didn't just say yes to a date, I put him on the spot and forced his hand into one!

I think.

Did I?

He said he wanted to take me out but didn't technically ask to take me out to lunch...

What the fuck is wrong with me?!

"Earth to Hope!" Katy screams, bringing me back.

"What?" I ask.

They both look at me in disbelief.

Ginny breaks the silence, "Are you actually going to go through with this?"

I pause, not sure how to respond. Should I tell them he

didn't *actually* ask me out to lunch? *Damn it. Did I strong-armed him into this? Fuck!* "That depends entirely on him," I reply, "he didn't *technically* ask me out..." I trail off at their expressions.

"What do you mean 'technically'?" Katy asks.

I sigh and flop down in the backseat of the car, waiting for them to get in the front while I think about how to answer that. "I *mean* that he didn't ask me, I kinda invited myself?" *Ugh.* "The last bit of the conversation you guys saw and heard, I basically *told* him he's taking me out. He didn't *ask*...I mean... he did say he wanted to take me out on a date and even asked if I wanted to go to Waffle House with him tonight, but he didn't actually ask me to lunch or anything..." I stop talking as I look up to their incredulous stares before they burst out laughing at my ramblings.

After they regain control, Ginny looks at me and says, "Hope. Honey. He may not have said 'will you go out with me,' but he definitely asked you on a Waffle House date."

We delve into the semantics of what happened, and they both questioned me about the rest of the time we spent together. I deftly deflect. I'm not opening that particular can of worms until I've had time to process what the hell just happened. I told them it was good, and left it at that. They didn't buy it. Not that it was bad or anything, they just thought there was more to it... and there was.

I'm not discussing *that* particular tidbit of information just yet.

He's a Daddy, and he wants me to be his submissive. What in the ever-loving fuck am I supposed to do with that information? I don't understand why he would ask me, a total stranger and an average-looking woman at best. I'm curious, don't get me wrong, I'm flattered he approached at all, but *what the hell...*

Am I seriously considering this?

Yes. Yes, I am.

By the time I get home, I've been silently contemplating a Google search of all things related to kink and Daddy Doms, but ultimately decide against it. The internet is a freaky place and I don't want to see something I can't unsee. I'd rather Landon teach me what he's interested in than do a deep dive and end up terrified.

Satisfied with my decision, I crawl into bed and start to unwind. My night with the girls was a blast, but I'm so glad to be back home. Just as I begin to drift, my phone goes off on the nightstand. It's well past midnight by now, so I check it to make sure it's not one of the girls saying they need a tow or my parents saying something is wrong with Lizzie.

Landon: Hey, it's Landon! I just wanted to shoot you a text and check that you made it home safely. I enjoyed meeting you tonight, I had a great time. Really looking forward to our date. Sweet Dreams!

Oohhh, he is so sweet!

Me: Hey! I made it home. Thank you for checking. I had a great time tonight too, and I'm excited to meet up again. Goodnight!

I put my phone back on the nightstand, lie down, and close my eyes. I can still feel the smile on my face as I drift off to sleep, thinking about Landon and what it would feel like to be his.

***

The Next Morning

I pull up to my parents' house. It's my childhood home. Two stories, finished basement, and so many memories. Thank

God for my parents. They've helped so much since Matt died. That's not to say my in-laws don't, they just live farther away and it takes *a lot* to plan a visit with them. My parents live so close to Lizzie and me, it kinda seems like I did it on purpose — I didn't, but hey, happy accidents!

Mama opens the garage door for me, and I walk in. Since I was out so late last night, they let Lizzie sleep over, and I'm so grateful. When I walk in, Lizzie is eating lunch, and I take a second to absorb the moment. She's so content, eating her peanut butter and banana sandwich with her apple juice. My dad is sitting next to her, talking to her while keeping the dog, Hank, away from the table and the scraps Lizzie is trying to feed him. She lets out a happy squeal that melts me inside when she sees me. She's growing up so fast, and in moments like this, I wish Matt could see her. See how big she is now, how smart she's become, how beautiful she is with her big blue-green eyes.

"Hey there, nugget! Have you had a good day?" I ask her.

She babbles back to me, throwing in some of her new and favorite words.

"Hi mama! You okay? Eat?"

"I'm alright, baby. Mama will eat when we get home."

"Daddy home?" She asks, and my heart drops out of my body completely.

My parents pause, giving me sympathetic stares. Choking down the tears and bracing against the stabbing in my heart, I kneel down and try to explain to my two-year-old why her daddy isn't at home.

"Daddy isn't home, baby. Daddy went to Heaven. We'll have to wait a while before we get to see him again."

"Okay. You okay?" She doesn't really understand, I mean,

she's two. Most adults have a hard time grasping the concept of Heaven.

Leaning into her, "No, baby. Mommy isn't okay yet, but she will be."

I don't want to lie to her and tell her I'm alright when I'm not. Even if she doesn't get it, I don't want her to think bottling up your emotions is the healthy way to deal with them.

When I stand back up, my mom gives me one of those hugs only a mother can give and reassures me, "You're doing a great job."

It's all I can do not to laugh at the notion of me doing a good job, that I'm *not* royally fucking this up, so I just nod and look away. I don't feel like I'm doing a good job. I feel like I'm letting her down. Like I'm letting Matt down. *Fuck* I hate this feeling. I need to get home and lie down. I need to do *something* to take my mind off everything wrong in my world. Coming back to myself, I sit at the table with my parents.

"So how was she last night?"

It's a standard question every time I pick her up. And in return, I get the standard answer.

"She was great! We played with her stethoscopes, read books, and watched Ms. Rachel. We even danced around in the yard with the neighbors when we went for a walk with Hank!"

I nod to show that I heard her, but in reality, my mind is on last night. Specifically, Landon. I haven't stopped thinking about him.

Why can't I stop thinking about him?

I mean, sure, he's handsome, with a strong jaw sharp enough to cut steel, piercing blue eyes, and a strong frame. It's no wonder I can't stop. But I think it might be more than that, more than what he said he wanted us to be. He was right, our conversation was easy — like we had done it a thousand times instead of once.

As if my quickly spiraling thoughts conjured the man himself, my phone vibrates.

"That Ginny and Katy?" Mama asks.

I guess the slight flush that spreads across my face gives me away because she immediately follows up with, "Who is he?"

Dad, bless him for trying, decides to go with, "How do you know that came from a 'he'? That could've been anyone. Someone from her new job even!"

Good looking out, Dad. The eternal optimist. I haven't even had my interview yet!

Too bad that mama knows better. She just gives him a look; you know the one? The one that kindly asks if you're stupid? The non-verbal, *bless your heart,* if you will.

As if to prove me right, she smiles at him and says, "Bless your heart, Jace. It's a good thing I love you." Then she turns her x-ray vision on me.

Here it comes.

With an excited expression, she repeats herself. "Who is he?"

"Just someone I met while the girls and I were out last night. We hit it off and exchanged numbers."

Mama narrows her eyes. I know she wants more details, but too bad for her. I'm not giving any.

You know those criminal investigative shows? How the cop sits there across from the suspect in the interrogation scenes and they wait each other out to see who will cave first?

It's me. I cave first.

"Alright! Alright! We agreed to have lunch today. But I want to spend time with my Lizzie the rest of the weekend, so I'm going to reschedule for next weekend."

Cue *the look.*

"I promise, I won't cancel on him! I'd like to go on Saturday afternoon, if you guys are able to watch her?"

Dad doesn't say anything, and I can't tell if he's excited about the idea of me going on a date again or not, daddy's little girl and all. Mama, however, is beaming. "Of course we'll watch her! She can spend the night with us Saturday night so you can get to church Sunday morning without rushing around to get her ready."

Well, now that that's settled, I guess there's no reason to put off looking at my phone.

Landon: Hey beautiful, I had a great time talking last night. When would you like to get lunch today? I'm free pretty much all afternoon.

Me: Hey, I'm glad you texted. I was wondering if we could push lunch to next Saturday? My daughter spent the night with my parents last night, and I wanted to spend the rest of the weekend with her before my interview on Monday.

Me: I'm so sorry. I understand if you don't want to wait.

Landon: Hey, hey, hey. Don't go convincing yourself of something like that. I don't mind waiting, and while I don't have kids of my own, I understand that family comes first. Always. Don't ever apologize for that.

Landon: Next Saturday should be fine. I'll know by

Wednesday what work will look like for the rest of the week and whether I'll have to go in. Is that okay with you?

Me: Yeah, that works. Thanks for being understanding.

Landon: Anytime, beautiful. Good luck at your interview, you're gonna kill it.

Me: LOL, you hardly know me. I could have a shit work ethic and blow it to hell.

Landon: Nah, I know enough ;)

I can't help it. I smile. Mama catches it and gives me a knowing grin. *Crap.*

Lizzie smiles up at me, and I pull her into my lap, snuggling close. She wraps her little arms around my neck and squeezes. She gives the best hugs! Picking her up, I start to head out when mom calls, "Good luck in your interview! I love you! See you next week!"

CHAPTER 4

Landon

It's only been a couple days since I saw her last. *Hope.* I can't believe the hold she has on me. I've never felt such a connection before, let alone so quickly. It sounds ridiculous, even in my own head. Our conversations were seamless and engaging, and I can't seem to get images of her out of my head.

Is it truly a connection or is it just a lusty trick of the mind?

All fucking weekend, I've walked around with my cock at half-mast. Nights are the worst — when I don't have anything else to occupy my mind — that's when she has free rein.

Every night, I've spent extra time in the shower with every fantasy of her I've conjured in my mind, explicit and innocent alike. It doesn't seem to matter, as long as she's there, I'm aching. *Her*, splayed over my knee, the creamy skin of her ass red and marred with my handprint. *Her*, sitting in my lap enjoying an ice cream cone on a hot day. *Her*, naked in my shower, water running down her luscious curves, chasing the soap in rivulets over her hips…

Shit! Get it together!

Just then, a singular knock sounds on my open door before James walks in. Nothing kills the hard-on I'm sporting like the face of my best friend walking in the door.

Thank you, James!

He comes waltzing into my office like he owns the damn place, plops down in the chair in front of my desk, and narrows his eyes on me.

Damn. He knows me too well.

"You sly fucker. You still have that same dopey expression on your face from Friday night! You got her number, but did you seal the deal?"

I don't like him asking about Hope that way. "Wouldn't you like to know?"

"I would, so spill it. Who is this woman that has managed to capture the attention of the *elusive Landon Reed* of Reed Enterprises?" He asks with a shit-eating grin on his face.

I roll my eyes. "Shut up, asshole. I can't believe that fucking article. I'm not elusive! Just because I wouldn't fuck the interviewer, I'm elusive? What even was her name? I probably should've reported her for harassment when I had the chance."

What I don't tell him is that I could've sworn I had seen the aforementioned interviewer across the street from the office last week, but I'm probably just confusing someone else as her. It's not the first time I thought I had seen her though. I feel like I'm losing my mind with how often it seems like she pops up. I swear I've even seen her at the grocery store down the street from my house, but I can't remember specific features, let alone her name, so I've never approached to find out.

James lets out a chuckle, shaking me from my inner turmoil. "I don't remember. But dude, you've barely dated anyone in *years*. The dates you have been on, are just because you're bored and wanted a little company. You're a little elusive."

Okay maybe I haven't seriously dated, I'll give him that,

but that doesn't make me a recluse! I was busy making sure our startup actually started up and didn't come crashing down around our ears. I decide to let it go and change the subject.

"You prepped for the interview today? She passed HR's check and the first two rounds of interviews without faltering."

James isn't stupid, he knows what I'm doing, but he doesn't call me on it. "Yeah I'm ready. I've got her file right here. The girl has all the credentials to be more than our secretary. I'd like to know why she's going for a position she's so over-qualified for."

Well, that's news to me. "Let me see her file."

He hands it over to me, and the name gives me pause. That name brings to mind the sultry images of *her* to the forefront.

Hope Lawson. Surely, it's a coincidence. This can't be *my* Hope. The Hope I was fantasizing about not even 15 minutes ago. The one I'm taking to lunch on Saturday. The same Hope I'm bound and determined to make just as hooked on me as I already am on her.

My intercom buzzes, breaking me from my thoughts.

The front desk clerk comes over the line, "Mr. Reed, Hope Lawson is here for her interview."

No time like the present! Let's get this show on the road.

"Send her up please. We're ready for her."

A few moments later, the elevator whirs, going down to pick up Mrs. Lawson. I'm proud of everything I've accomplished. This whole building is mine. Well, mine and James'. Reed Enterprises is a fast-growing real estate agency. With James as our top agent and co-founder, and me behind the scenes as the CEO, we get the top pick of lots. Clients love us for our diverse selection of agents and their comprehensive knowledge of all things home-buying. The homes we're known to sell aren't just cookie-cutter homes though.

James and I started flipping houses in college. Our parents gave us a loan for our first project, and after paying them back, we took what remained of our profits and did it again. And again. And again. And now, we're one of the most sought-after companies in the state for our ability to make our clients' dream home a reality.

My thoughts come back to the interview when I hear the elevator announce its arrival. At first, I can't see anything but the doors opening. Then I hear the muted clicking of heels on the carpeted flooring. I start to glance up, only to pause at the expanse of leg I see through my office window under the half-drawn blinds. They're nice legs, shapely and full. I can see the bottom hemline of her black pencil skirt, and my eyes are fixated on it as she rounds the corner of my office door.

I carefully trek my way up, following the line of curves along her thighs to her full, wide hips. Hips that look very familiar...hips I've been dreaming about while rutting into my bed as I sleep like a damn teenage boy. I keep going, over the dip in her waist, visually caressing the curve of her breasts to land on the glacial eyes that have haunted my dreams all damn weekend long.

Well, this may have gotten complicated.

I meet her shocked eyes and fully take her in. Her makeup is minimal, but professional. Her eyes lined only along the top, lashes coated in mascara, and her lips are painted a color like red wine to accent the army green blouse buttoned up her front. If I thought casual Hope was beautiful, professional Hope is a wet fucking dream. The loose-fitted blouse doing nothing to disguise her curves, and the skirt is so snug across her hips and ass that I can't help but notice the lack of a panty line.

James looks back and forth between us with a confused look on his face before it dawns on him, and he grins. *Great.*

"Hello, Mrs. Lawson. My name is James Monroe. I'm the co-founder of Reed Enterprises and will be joining in on this interview if that's alright with you."

Hope puts on a professional smile. Looking at James, she holds out her hand and replies, "Of course, it's wonderful to meet you. And it's Ms., not Mrs. anymore."

The hitch in her voice when she corrects James makes me furrow my brow. So, she was married, and it seems she's still upset about the change...interesting.

He doesn't let go of her hand right away, it's just a beat too long to be considered professional, *the fucker*. He's messing with me, trying to get me to react.

Turning to me, she holds her smile firmly in place and sticks out her hand, "Hi there, I'm Hope Lawson. Mr. Reed, I presume?"

I didn't notice Friday night because of the noise, but it sounds like she has a slight southern accent she's trying to downplay. I look from her outstretched hand to her eyes, silently pleading with me to play along.

Fine, I will. We can play by her rules...to *a degree.*

Reaching for her hand, I smile and reply, "Yes, I'm Mr. Reed." She looks relieved. "But since you know me as Landon, why don't we skip the formalities?" She blanches a little, shocked by my blatant acknowledgement that we already know each other.

James chokes on a laugh trying, and failing, to cover it with a cough. Hope cuts her narrowed eyes to him before she catches herself, remembering she's in an interview.

Oh, this is going to be fun.

CHAPTER 5

Hope

Shit. Shit. Shit. Shit. Shit.

Landon is the owner of Reed Enterprises?! Why didn't I do an image-related search last night after Lizzie went down?! Too late now, I guess. And he just outed me to the co-owner!

Double shit.

I look between them at a loss for what to say or do. Making up my mind, I stand taller, give a slight nod, and say, "I apologize for not recognizing you sooner. I should have. I understand if there's a conflict of interest. Thank you for your time all the same."

I turn to leave, but barely make a half-turn out the door before familiar calloused hands gently grip my elbow. Turning, I look at the face of the man who has haunted my dreams since Friday night. And I mean *haunted*. I keep imagining that I can feel the heat of his body next to me, like it was in the booth of the bar, and it's utterly maddening.

"Hope, please don't go. We're not laughing at you, and I'm not offended you didn't know who I was. Quite the opposite. It was a huge relief to speak to someone as Landon and not Landon Reed, 'Real Estate mogul'." He rolls his eyes at the moniker. "Have a seat, let's get your interview started. From the looks of your resume, this will merely be a formality."

***

"Well, Hope, I don't have any other questions, and I honestly think you'll be a great fit here with us."

"Thank you, Mr. Monroe. I really appreciate that. It means a lot from someone as accomplished as yourself."

A quiet huff sounds from Landon, and when I cut my eyes over he looks...jealous, maybe, as he glares at Mr. Monroe from the corner of his eye. *Weird.*

Mr. Monroe waves a hand, "Please, call me James. I wouldn't care for the formality even if you weren't friends with Landon." Turning to give the man himself a devilish smirk.

I nod and look over at him.

Dammit.

I just *knew* he'd fill out a complete suit like it was tailored for him. Considering how well Reed Enterprises has done over the last five years, it probably was. The buttons on his shirt strain every time he takes a deep breath, as if he were savoring the smell of warm chocolate chip cookies. I come back to the real world when I see his mouth move, more than hear him say, "I have two more questions for you, Hope."

"Alright, let's hear them."

"First, why would you pick a job you are clearly overqualified for?"

I narrow my eyes on him, then glance at James, who appears curious but is at least polite enough not to ask. Looking back at Landon, my response is short and curt. "Flexibility."

Landon nods in understanding before he continues. "Secondly, do you understand that giving you this position is in no way, shape, or form favoritism? And you also understand that we will still be going to lunch on Saturday?"

I am completely and utterly stunned.

Not only is he implying that I got the job, but he has the audacity to hold me to our date as if our dynamics didn't just get turned on their head.

And in front of his business partner!

I can feel the flush climbing as I openly glare at Landon for embarrassing me like this. Before I can lash out though, James stands to excuse himself. "Hope, it was wonderful to meet you." I rise to meet him, "And I look forward to working with you." He steps closer and drops his voice, his brown eyes alight with humor, "Go easy on him. I can see you're angry and probably a little embarrassed being put on the spot like this, but I've never seen him like this before. Ever. He's been in his head all weekend over you. He really likes you, and he wants it all." Dropping his voice further and arching a brow to tell me he *knows*, "All of it."

Just when I thought I couldn't be more embarrassed.

Shocked into silence, I simply nod to acknowledge him. He walks past me, and suddenly I'm left alone with Landon for the first time all weekend. He stands up to round his desk, and before I can do anything other than take a breath, he kisses me.

He. Kisses. Me.

It's not just *any* kiss though. No, it's one of those heart-stopping, toe-curling, earth-shattering kisses. The kind where you feel your soul leave your body, stand back, and watch it happen. Before I know it, I'm falling into the kiss. I kiss him back just as hard and as passionately as he's kissing me. I hear a moan fall between us before either one of us can swallow it down, and I think it came from me.

Fuck he's good at this. This is the kind of kiss you read about in all those wonderfully raunchy smutty books, the kind that dampens your panties when you think about it later.

Speaking of which, mine are soaked.

Landon spins me around and pushes me to lean against his desk. His hands grip my face like a lifeline and mine have worked their way over his arms to his shoulders. Starting at his calloused fingertips and gliding up the forearms that have no business being as defined and veiny as they are, over his bulging biceps as he moves to wrap me in his arms and lightly squeeze, across shoulders so broad and strong he could carry me across them without breaking a sweat or huffing a breath, and up into those lusciously thick waves. I tangle my fingers there and give a little tug. He grunts in response and pulls me tighter to his sculpted chest as he runs his hands down my back to roughly squeeze my ass.

That's what breaks the spell. I pull away, quickly looking at the lipstick smeared across his mouth.

My lipstick.

Holy fucking shitballs. I just tongue fucked my boss.

And I loved every second.

CHAPTER 6
Landon

That. Kiss.

Holy hot damn.

That kiss!

That kiss was *everything*. Every ounce of passion I've been looking for in a partner, both in life and play. If I had any doubts before, they're gone now.

She. Is. *MINE*. I don't even care how possessive that sounds.

And I'm already dying for another hit. One kiss and I'm fucking addicted. One kiss and she has me wrapped around her little finger. One kiss and I need more. More of her taste, her sounds, her nails along my scalp.

Just *her*.

Her panicked babbling pulls me out of my head. "...I can't believe I just did that. We can't do that. This can't happen again. *We* can't happen." She pauses long enough to whirl on me. "Why are you just standing there? Say something!"

I can't help it.

I laugh.

Hard.

Once I have some semblance of control over myself again, I look into her narrowed eyes, cradle her cheeks, and kiss her again. This one is more chaste. Giving a little nip at the end as a promise for more. Her face is flushed from our heated touches and from the anger I can still see simmering behind her eyes. She pushes off me and tries to step away again.

"Baby girl, I'm only so patient. You can't keep walking away from me without permission."

She audibly gasps. Her jaw dropping open just enough for me to imagine filling that scrumptious mouth of hers. She starts to sputter out a response before I place my finger over her lips, leaning in to give another teasing nip. This time, she leans in too.

"Hope, baby girl, I need you to listen to me, okay? Can you do that for Daddy?"

Her breath hitches in her chest, and she nods.

"No, Hope. I need words. Use your words, sweetheart."

A whispered "yes," is her response.

We'll work on it.

I kiss her forehead, "Good girl," she shudders. "Here is how this is going to play out, if you're still interested. Are you still interested?"

She nods again, forgetting to use her words.

I grab her chin with my thumb and forefinger, gently reminding her, "This is the last time I'm going to tell you, Hope. Use your words. Every time. Unless I tell you otherwise. If you can't follow Daddy's directions, I will punish you. And I would really prefer to wait for that, as much as we would both enjoy it."

Her pupils are blown so wide there's barely anything left of the glacial blue except a tight ring. She begins to nod her head again before I raise my brow and she catches herself, "Yes."

"Yes, what?"

"Yes, I'm still interested."

"Good, but that's not what I want to hear, baby girl."

She looks confused for half a second before it hits her. I can see her nostrils flare, and I swear I can *smell* her arousal. She only pauses for the briefest moment, and it's enough to make my heart stutter in my chest, before she replies.

"Yes, Daddy. I'm still interested."

I can't bite back my groan, and I dive in to seal her words with my lips, tasting them on her.

Tasting her.

I drive myself to the edge from nothing more than her mouth on mine. *I am so fucked.* Forcibly pulling myself away, I put an arm's length between us, and she starts to lean in before righting herself.

We need to talk first.

"We need to talk for a minute to make sure we're on the same page, but we need to clean up first." I point her to the left of my floor-to-ceiling bookcase. "There's a bathroom through there."

When she steps through and closes the door behind her, I take a deep breath. I can still smell her perfume. Vanilla and something warm and earthy. Like cookies and coffee in fall. I take another breath to breathe her in as I reach for the tissues on my desk to wipe my mouth.

Focus.

She opens up the bathroom door and appears almost back to normal, aside from her kiss-swollen lips that now lack the color from when she first walked in. She's even more stunning now. Ethereal. There are no words that describe how beautiful she is, standing in my office, waiting for what I have to say, like the good girl she is.

Time to figure out where we go from here.

CHAPTER 7

Hope

I stand in his office dumbstruck, because *that just happened*.

I kissed my boss.

I let him call me 'baby girl' and 'sweetheart'…I called him 'Daddy'.

Fuck. That was so fucking hot. The way he took charge, commanding the room and my attention with so few words. With one demand; that I use my words to verbally acknowledge the conversation and to express my enthusiastic consent to what was happening.

This is it. That little voice in the back of my head starts piping up. *This is what I've been missing since Matt died.*

Did I say I sometimes like that voice? *Yeah, well, she's a dumb bitch.*

I shouldn't want this! With my boss no less!

"Hey, Hope. Come back to me, baby. Focus on me." His voice drags me back to where I am. Standing in his office, in his arms, with his focus solely on me.

"I'm here," I whisper. I can't seem to manage much more than that.

With probing eyes he orders, "Come here."

He pulls me over to the overstuffed deep chocolate colored leather couch and sits me down. He walks over to a wet bar that I didn't notice in the corner by the floor-to-ceiling bookshelf that I *also* didn't notice. I was completely zeroed in on him, unable to pay attention to the room around me. Now that I've had a second to take a breath that wasn't completely saturated with his scent, I could appreciate the homey feel with the nod to days gone by with the inclusion of the wet bar.

His view is something else though.

I'm not much for city views, but I can appreciate beauty when I see it. I remember traveling through on family vacations when I was little. The city looks incredible lit up in the dark, lights of all colors at all different heights make "The City in the Forest" light up like a Christmas tree. I've lived in Georgia my whole life. My dad worked out of Atlanta for the same number of years that I've been on this earth.

I've seen Atlanta.

I've walked the streets, seen the sights, been there, done that, got the t-shirt. But I've never seen it like this. The office sat in the middle of Atlantic Station, tall enough that from his office's wall-to-wall windows, Landon had a view of *everything*. The skyline framed in the windows before me was like nothing else. Structures all around, some of them covered in commissioned art, others in graffiti, but altogether making the city what it is.

It was impressive, bordering on opulent.

Landon comes back over to me with a glass of what smells like whiskey, and despite the hour, I take a sip. I need something to calm my frazzled nerves. He sits down, very close. I'm about to move to the side to make room when he reaches one arm under my legs and the other behind me to haul me into his lap. Seated on my perch, I look at him, slack-jawed and try to shift next to him again.

He *growls.*

Or at least, that's what it sounds like when he bites out, "Don't."

His tone makes me pause before he buries his nose in my hair, kisses my neck, and inhales deeply, scenting me like some sort of beast. Pulling back, he appears calmer when he apologizes.

"Sorry, baby girl. I like having you on my lap, having my hands on you. I much prefer to have you here than next to me."

I start to protest, "Landon, don't be silly, I can't sit on your lap, I'm too heavy..."

At his sharp inhale, I cut off. Shocked, and a little unnerved to see the fire blazing in his eyes when he demands, "Who the *hell* told you that?"

I shake my head, "No one, but I know what the scale says. And what the doctor loves to reiterate to me when I go see him."

Landon lets out a long breath, seeming to garner the strength to end this conversation. "Sweetheart, you're not too heavy. You're absolutely perfect. If you have any doubts..." he pauses to grind his pelvis into my ass, forcing a gasp from my lips.

Shit, he's big. And thick.

"...forget about them. Believe me when I tell you every inch of you is utter perfection." He gives my hips a squeeze as if to prove his point further.

Blushing and smiling, I drop my gaze, but he isn't having

any of that. "Give me those eyes, gorgeous. I want you to see the truth in mine when we have this conversation."

"I want you. I think I've made that pretty clear. I want to take you on dates, I want to hold your hand, kiss your lips, and brush that stray hair behind your ear," he adds with a chuckle, moving the piece back in place. "I don't care that you work as our secretary; there's nothing in the company policy that bans office relationships. As long as productivity isn't affected, James and I don't care."

Jumping right into the deep end, I see.

I start to argue that he should care about the implications when he says, "I can already see the arguments building behind your eyes. Please, don't outright reject the idea of us. I know you feel something too. If it'll make you feel better, I can have Diana in HR draft up a relationship disclosure of sorts that will protect your job should anything happen between us. But let me tell you now, I'm serious about us, Hope. I don't plan on letting you go without a fight."

Once again, I'm left utterly speechless.

It seems he's really given this some thought, and he has taken the only arguments I had in my head and offered a solution. I don't want to give up on whatever this is. I like the connection we seem to have, and hell, if that kiss is anything to go by, we have sexual chemistry out the ass and would be explosive in bed.

And I must say, his lap is quite comfortable. Even with all of that, there's still the power dynamic in play that worries me. He's my boss, even with some sort of disclosure in place to protect us, I don't love the idea of our business being known by all in the office. It would make it look like I just fucked my way into the position.

Landon interrupts my inner thoughts with another completely logical solution.

"Look at me, angel."

When I do he continues, "I know you can see how serious I am, and I feel like there might be something holding you back. This is a lot; a new relationship, a new job, taking care of Lizzie. Take the week to think. I'll have Diana draw up the papers for you to look over by Wednesday. She'll send them over with our official offer. You'll start onboarding on Monday, and we can go over any questions you have about us on our date on Saturday." He pauses to look at me, making sure I'm following. "Does that sound like a plan, baby girl?"

My response sounds as relieved as I feel, "Yes, thank you for understanding."

I'm fucking putty in his hands with all these damn endearments.

"Of course, baby girl. I want to give you everything."

In a daze, I get up to leave, feeling better than I have in a long time while simultaneously nervous about the exact same thing that makes me feel so calm.

Doesn't mean I can't torture him a bit though.

Grinning, I turn back when I reach the door. I give a wink and a sugary sweet, "See you Saturday...Daddy."

I exit his office full-on smiling to myself at his tortured groan, taking extra care to throw a little sway in my walk.

CHAPTER 8
Landon

It's Wednesday and I'm twitchy as hell.

After Hope left, the front desk called to say a package had been delivered. It was weird since no one had ordered anything to be sent to the office. When it was brought up, I opened the long rectangular box to find a single rose. That was it. No note, nothing else in the box. An uneasy shiver went down my spine as I threw the box away. I haven't contacted Hope since the interview Monday morning to give her space to think, and I'm starting to regret that decision. I don't want to push too hard, but I don't want her to think I've forgotten about her either.

Just call her. Keep it short and sweet.

After several moments of internal debate, I pick up my phone to call Hope. I need to hear her voice if I can't see her yet.

Dialing, I wait while it rings. And rings. And rings. On the fourth, her voicemail picks up. I can't help the sting of disappointment at not getting to talk to her, but her voicemail greeting is sweet and makes me smile.

"Hey y'all! You've reached Hope Lawson. Be sure to leave a message, and I'll call you back when I can. Have a blessed day!"

beep

Shit! I didn't want to leave a voicemail!

Did I?

Well, it'll seem weird if I don't say anything now that it's recording.

"H-hey, Hope. It's Landon. I wanted to call and see how your day was going. Call me back if you can. I can't wait to see you this weekend. Bye."

There. Done. That wasn't so bad.

My phone rings, and I get excited for two seconds before it clicks in my brain that it's my desk phone, not my cell. Shaking my head at myself, I pick it up to answer.

"Landon Reed."

"Hello, Mr. Reed. This is Diana down in HR. I'm calling about the new hire contract and offer you had me review and send."

I put the proposal together myself; everything should be in order.

"Yes, hey Di. How can I help? Did you have a question?"

"Yes, sir, I did. I just wanted to clarify a few things."

What could she have a question about?

"Please, continue."

"I see that the salary offer is well above average for a secretary in this field. Is that number correct, or do I need to make edits and send them to you for approval?"

"No, it's correct. Mr. Monroe and I have decided that, based on her education and experience, we'll be giving her more than the average secretarial duties to complete and wanted to compensate her fairly."

"Perfect. Thank you for the clarity on that. Next would be the disclosure you had me draw up."

I can all but hear the hesitation and question in her voice. If Diana hadn't worked with us as long as she had, I'd be a little offended at the tone. Diana is probably just curious. This is rather out of character for me.

I sigh, "Alright, Di. Ask your questions. And enough with the formal bullshit, please."

She huffs out a laugh, "Alright, fine. Who is she, Landon? And if you're already involved, why am I just now finding out, and why are we offering her a job? Can you say nepotism?!"

I should've seen this coming.

Shaking my head, I give her the truth.

"Hope and I met last Friday at a bar, completely by chance. She didn't know who I was, and I didn't know her. She came to the office Monday morning for her interview and tried to back out before James and I convinced her to go through with it. Ultimately, she's the best candidate for the job, and she'll even be helping more than the average person in this position because of her skillset." I sigh and go on, "Yes, I'm attracted to her. And yes, I'm taking her out on Saturday, but none of that impacted our decision, I swear. She truly is a perfect fit."

"Alright, Landon. I'll take your word, but tread lightly. Be smart."

That's Diana for you. Always looking out for us. "Thanks, Di. I will."

"Want me to go ahead and send this out?"

Grinning like the Cheshire Cat, an idea starts to take shape, "No, thank you though. Send everything to me. And find me her address, please."

I can all but hear Diana rolling her eyes as I hang up the phone. Looks like I get to see my girl after all.

***

Rolling up outside the single-story ranch style home, I'm hit with a possessive urge.

Is this the home she had with him?

Did she cuddle close on the couch with him here? Obviously, dipshit. They had a daughter together.

Is this where they brought Lizzie home together, happy and exhausted?

I try hard to dial it back, I really do, but I can't help the twinge of bitterness. I know I can't begrudge her the life she had before me, and I don't. That life brought her to me, but it doesn't stop the feeling. I shake my head at my own irrationality as I get out of the car. Walking up the driveway, I take in the house and yard. It's well-kept; the yard neatly trimmed, flowers in bloom along the walkway, and the siding is clean.

Huh.

I thought she was a single mom. Not to stereotype or anything, but I didn't think she would have a lot of time to do this kind of thing. Filing that away for later, I continue up the front porch and knock on the door. I don't even know if she's home, and if she is home and Lizzie is sleeping, I don't want to wake her up.

Through the door, I can hear the pattering of little feet and happy squeals. I can't help but smile at the noise. *I really do love kids.* I didn't think about potentially meeting Lizzie when I got this idea. I was so focused on seeing Hope again. I need to do better to remember that Hope isn't the only one in this relationship. I knock on the door and hear the deadbolt being thrown back before the door cracks open and Hope peeks out. She stands there, shocked to see me, before cracking open the door a little more.

Hesitantly, she says, "H-hey Landon." She pauses, looking around. "What are you...? How did...?"

She stops to gather herself, "Not that I'm not happy to see you, but what are you doing here? How do you know where I live?" She looks down at herself before her eyes fly wide and she flushes a deep red. "And why didn't you call me to tell me you were coming?!"

At her outburst, I take her in.

Her face is free of any trace of makeup, not that she wore much to begin with. Her hair is up in a messy bun— the kind that you can tell was a rush job just to get it out of her face instead of the kind I've seen girls spend more than three seconds on. She's wearing a ratty, old t-shirt that's literally falling apart at the seams, and a pair of spanx over an ass that's *much* fuller than I previously thought. Her feet are bare on the hardwood floors with her toes painted a pretty, pale pink. I slowly bring my eyes back to her face to see her standing there, taking me in just as thoroughly as I had done her.

She shocks herself back to the present when her eyes meet mine, and she repeats her question. "What are you doing here?"

"I came by to bring you the offer and the contract to review and sign. I was on this side of town anyway."

Liar.

Her narrowed eyes and quirked brow tell me she doesn't buy it. So, I smile and shrug. She rolls her eyes and opens the door wider, arching a brow silently asking if I want to come in.

"Let's not pretend I buy that." She says as she steps to the side. "What are you really doing here, and how do you know where I live?"

I run my hand along the back of my neck, feeling a little embarrassed the more I think about my impulsive decision. Sighing, "I wanted to see you. I called, but you didn't answer. Diana, my HR rep, called me to finalize your paperwork and I had her send it to me along with your address before she emailed it, so I could see you. A-are you mad?"

She just stands there, not saying anything.

Damn. Too far, Landon.

I start to back toward the door I just walked through, "I'm so sorry, I shouldn't have done that."

She shakes her head, but at the low growl under my breath, she remembers to use her words. "No, I'm not mad. I feel like I should be, but I'm not. Just surprised." She has a slight blush to her cheeks as she continues, "I think it's kinda sweet actually."

Before I can move, a blur of blonde hair whirls into the room. She slams into her mother with a peal of giggles that has me downright giddy inside. She stops when she notices me standing there and hides behind her mom. Hope smiles and gives a little shake of her head as she looks at the little girl. Bending over to pick her up, she puts her on her hip.

Hope looks at the little girl, and glances at me, "Lizzie, this is mommy's friend Mr. Landon. Can you say 'hello'?" Lizzie looks at Hope and back at me before lowering her face, looking a little on the shy side.

Hope looks back up at me with a soft smile I haven't seen before and apologizes for Lizzie's shyness, "Sorry, she's actually very social. I didn't plan on introducing the two of you yet. I was going to wait until after this weekend to decide."

I shake my head to reassure her that her apologies aren't necessary. "It's okay, she doesn't know me, though I do hope to change that. I truly am sorry to have popped over like this; I didn't even stop to think about Lizzie being here. Will you forgive me?"

"Already forgotten."

The way she looks at her daughter, with unadulterated and unconditional love, melts my heart toward her even more. She doesn't even realize that she has it completely. I honestly didn't even realize someone could capture it so quickly, but my whole heart is hers, and therefore Lizzie's. I will protect this little girl as fiercely and devotedly as I will her mother.

We move further into the house and I begin to notice the toys lying around while I try my damnedest not to look at Hope's ass in those spanx.

She's trying to kill me.

I let out a sigh while thinking that it would be one hell of a way to go. Hope hears my sigh and turns a questioning look on me. I consider playing it off, but then I wouldn't get to see that cute blush of hers.

My voice is raspy as I pull her closer, "Baby girl, you're killing me in those shorts. I know how to control myself, so please don't feel like you have to put something else on — *believe me*, I'm enjoying the view — I was just thinking that dying between your splayed thighs while feasting on your dripping pussy would be my ideal way to go." Her blush is so dark and running so deep, I wonder if her nipples have flushed with the rest of her. At that thought my eyes drop, and I'm disappointed that I can't see them poking through the thin cotton.

She follows my gaze, a little tense, but then remembers she's covered and blows out a relieved breath. She looks back up at me with a slight grin on her face, one that tells me I'm about to be in trouble.

Oh boy.

She puts Lizzie down next to a pile of toys and *bends over* to arrange them in front of the toddler. Reaching for the remote, she puts something on the TV for background noise before turning back to me with a triumphant smile stretched across her lips. I look over her shoulder to make sure Lizzie is occupied before adjusting myself without any sort of shame, and I'm rewarded when I get to watch her eyes darken and her skin blister in goosebumps.

This isn't how I saw the afternoon going, but I am not mad.

Shaking ourselves from the suffocating, lust-filled haze choking the room, we return to the conversation.

"I really did bring the offer and contract. Where would you like me to put it?"

"Oh! So, you were serious? Awesome, you can just put it on the dining table. I'll look over everything tonight when Lizzie goes to bed."

"Sounds good."

I go to place the papers on the table and stop when I pass a wall of pictures. I see pictures of a younger Lizzie, being held by Hope. She is truly a stunning woman, even without the everyday getup someone puts on before leaving the house. As my eyes scan the pictures, I see one of Hope with a man looking down at her adoringly while she laughs at the camera.

This must be Matt.

He doesn't appear to be in any pictures taken within the last year, at least.

Why would he leave someone as perfect as Hope? And with Lizzie in the picture? And why does she still have a picture of her and her ex up on the wall?

I must've taken too long, because Hope comes rounding the corner calling my name with a smile in her voice, "Hey Landon, did you get..." Her words fizzle out, and she slows her steps, eyes wide with emotion.

Pain? Fear? Sadness? Instead of denying my snooping, albeit accidental, I ask, "This your ex?"

She visibly flinches and starts to curl in on herself. Shaking her head, she softly says, "Not my ex..."

I'm confused.

"You lost me, sweetheart. You said in your interview that you're a Ms. not a Mrs., so if he's not your ex..." That's when it hits me. No, he's not her ex.

Before I can think about it, I drop the papers on the ground with a flutter and pull her into a bone-crushing hug. She wraps her arms around me, her body shaking. It's not until I feel the dampness through my shirt that I realize she's crying. "Shhh, princess. I'm right here, okay?"

She nods, holding tighter.

"Will Lizzie be okay if we go to the kitchen?" She nods again.

"Come on, baby girl." Picking her up, I carry her down the hall and set her on the kitchen counter. I go through her cabinets looking for the glasses. Finding one, I fill it with water and hand it to her. Her hands shake as she reaches for the glass, taking a drink. When she seems to have gathered herself, she starts to speak.

"We were together for a long time before we got married.

About 6 years…"

She gets choked up, and I try to stop her.

"Hey, you don't owe…"

She shakes her head at me, "Yes, I do owe you an explanation. If you insist on getting involved in my life — our life," she says with a glance toward the living room, "then you need to know what you're asking for."

Pausing to take a fortifying breath, she goes on.

"We got married young; I was 23. We waited to have kids for about a year, but we were both ready for the next step. We were so excited to be parents, to raise a family. It happened pretty quickly, to be honest; we were lucky." She gives a humorless laugh, "Until we weren't. Like I said, we got pregnant with Lizzie quickly, and the pregnancy was normal and healthy. Birth is hard, no matter how you slice it, but it was overall a good experience. We were happy. We had everything we wanted." She smiles to herself, lost in memory, "He surprised me with this house one day. Brought Lizzie and me here, telling us 'This is it! This is the one!' I loved it, and we closed on it seemingly overnight. Moved in, got settled. Everything was perfect."

Her smile falls, and she drops her eyes as they start to glisten. "Matt was on his way home from work late one night. It didn't happen often, but when it did, it was usually even after I had gone to bed. Granted, I didn't stay up late very often since Lizzie was still getting up during the night for diaper changes." Another pause. When she looks back at me, her eyes are swimming with tears. "He died in a car accident. Drunk driver. Head on."

She doesn't give any details, and I don't ask. I just step between her legs and hold her close, letting her lose herself, even if for just a moment. Something tells me she doesn't let herself have many.

I thought she was done, but the last bit shatters my aching heart. "Lizzie's first birthday was five days later."

We both jump a little at the sound of pattering feet and the front door opening. I tense, immediately on the defensive as I run around the corner to grab Lizzie away from the door. Hope catches up before I can snatch up and scare the little girl, "It's okay, it's just my friends." I nod and blow out a breath to steady myself.

I look down at Lizzie and find her watching me. She toddles over and holds up her hands to me. Hope's mouth opens in shock, and when I look to her for permission, she nods.

Again, with the damn nods.

Sniffling and wiping her eyes, "I'm surprised. She doesn't usually warm up so quickly to someone, especially someone she's never met before. Even Ginny and Katy, and she's known them her whole life." She lifts her chin toward the door as it closes, "Watch. She'll say 'hi' to them but won't engage much beyond that until she warms up to them being in her space."

Sure enough, it plays out just like Hope said it would. When Lizzie sees the girls, she waves 'hello' and asks to be picked up again — only, not by Hope, but by me. I bend to pick up the little girl, and she burrows her face into my neck. Hope and I stand there staring at each other in stunned silence, too surprised to break the spell.

Ginny and Katy come into the house with a flourish.

"Honey, we're home! And you have a package on the front porch. What did you get?"

"Hey babe, where are you and the little princess? I've got her a..."

They trail off as they come to the living room where we're standing, staring at each other. Blatant shock on both their faces. I'm not sure whether that's from seeing me in Hope's house or from Lizzie in my arms.

Katy solves that for me though.

"Holy…She let…He…They're…What?" *They're shocked by both my presence and Lizzie being in my arms.*

Ginny watches me closely, eyes contemplating how to process the scene before her.

Hope steps in, "Girls, you remember Landon?"

They nod mutely.

Katy recovers first. "Good to see you, Landon. We didn't expect you to be here, otherwise we wouldn't have just walked in."

"No worries. I came to deliver the offer contract to Hope since I was in the area."

"Offer contract?" Ginny asks.

I look at Hope, and she gives herself a facepalm. "Sorry! I forgot to tell you girls. My interview on Monday? With Reed Enterprises?" She turns to me with a smile, "Hey Landon, what's your last name again?"

I laugh at her antics. "Reed."

CHAPTER 9

Hope

The girls inhale sharply at the shock and I flash them some jazz hands and a lighthearted, "Surprise! I swear, I was gonna tell y'all today when I saw you. I didn't plan on Landon showing up to drop off the offer though so…"

They look between us a few times before Katy grins. "That's great! You'll get to see each other all the time! Congrats on the job, babe!"

"Thanks, Katy."

I turn to Ginny, who hasn't said anything.

We've been friends forever, so she doesn't have to. I know what she needs to hear.

"Honestly Gin, I'm excited for both the job and my date with Landon. There's actually two pieces of paperwork. One is the offer, and the other is a disclosure-type document that has a clause in it that will protect my job if anything were to happen between Landon and me. It was all his idea, too," I say, gesturing to Landon, who is currently pretending he can't hear our conversation while talking to Lizzie.

The sight makes me pause. My eyes water and my breath hitches at how natural it looks, the two of them together. Ginny follows my gaze, and she softens.

Turning back to her and Katy, I gesture toward the kitchen.

As soon as we cross the threshold, I whirl, "He knows."

Both Ginny and Katy freeze.

"I told him about Matt, you guys walked in on the end of that conversation. Y'all have some timing, by the way. Anyway, he knows everything."

The girls look at each other, me, and then out toward the living room where we can hear Landon playing with Lizzie in the living room. There's a pregnant pause as I wait to hear what they have to say. And then I'm covering my ears from their squeals.

I guess they're okay with it.

We head back into the living room, where Landon is on the floor with Lizzie helping her build a tower with her blocks, and my heart stops. *It's just so damn cute!* The girls and I make our way over to the couch to settle in and watch them while the TV plays Bluey in the background. We've been sitting around talking for about an hour when Lizzie gets up and makes her way toward the entryway. When I move to stand, Landon tells me to sit and relax — that he doesn't mind going to bring her back in with us as long as it's okay with me. I give him the okay and am just leaning back against the couch when I hear him shout, "What the fuck?!"

I bolt up off the couch and cross the space in record time. When I swing around the corner, I see Landon holding Lizzie and an open box on the floor. I reach them, grabbing for Lizzie who is starting to squirm in Landon's arms, and take a step toward the box.

"Hope, please don't—" but it's too late. I can see inside the box, and I *really* wish I hadn't. My eyes water, and I start to retch. Inside the box is a fucking pig snout. Not one of those funny party favor things that you wear with a string around your head.

A. Real. Snout. I'm going to be sick.

I hand Lizzie back to Landon and bolt to the kitchen. *There's no way I'm making it to the bathroom.* I make it to the sink just in time to expel the coffee and granola bar I had earlier. I can vaguely hear Ginny and Katy in the front room trying to figure out what's going on as I continue to lose the little bit of food I had managed to eat so far today. When I finally stop dry heaving, I notice the feel of a large hand rubbing circles on my back and another holding my hair back.

I lock eyes with Landon over my shoulder and try to speak around my raw throat. I manage to choke out, "Lizzie..." and Landon reassures me.

"Ginny and Katy took her to her room to play. I came in here to check on you when they were all settled."

Nodding, I rest my head on my arms as I continue to lean over the sink and catch my breath.

"I'm going to grab you some water, baby girl. Will you be okay if I let your hair down?"

"I'll be fine, thank you. I'm so sorry." I reach up to turn on the sink to rinse it out. He grabs me another glass of water and comes back over, moving my hair back off my neck.

"Why are you apologizing, baby girl? You didn't do anything." He raises an eyebrow and cocks a slight smirk, "And I'm assuming you didn't order a pig snout."

I huff a laugh and shake my head as I reply, "No. Definitely not. That was vile."

His smirk falls, and his eyes cloud over, "I'm going to look for a return address. Why don't you call the police while I do?"

"That's probably a good idea."

Landon walks back toward the front door while I dial. The dispatch officer says they'll send someone out immediately to take a look. I thank them, hang up, and just stand there wondering what the hell is going on. I have no idea how long I'm lost in my thoughts until Landon steps into my field of vision, concern written all over his face.

"There you are. You didn't respond the first time I said your name and I got worried. Why don't we go sit in the living room? Are the police on their way?"

I nod my head and numbly walk across the kitchen to the couch. I can't help but shiver as we pass the entryway. Belatedly, I wonder if I'm going into shock. Landon sits me down and heads back to the kitchen, returning with my glass of water. I sip slowly, my thoughts racing, trying to think up a reason someone would send a pig snout to my house.

We sit in silence, Landon rubbing soothing circles on my back. I'm not sure how long we sat there, but eventually Ginny and Katy come back to the living room, telling me that Lizzie fell asleep while they were playing. I just keep nodding, still reeling over the events of the afternoon. The police finally show up, and one officer starts asking questions while his partner looks over the contents of the box. When the officer asks me if I have any enemies or if I've upset anyone recently, I vehemently shake my head.

"Officer, that's just not possible. I'm a widowed mother. My daughter goes to preschool two days a week, and I've been working part-time at a coffee shop for the last few months as I readjust. My parents watch my daughter on the days I have to work."

"Okay, ma'am. Thank you for the information. I'm so sorry for what you've had to go through today, and I'm sorry for your loss." He hands me a card. "Call if you can think of anything, no matter how small."

"Of course, thank you both for coming out here so quickly."

Landon steps forward, "Let me walk you out."

When Landon comes back in, he appears to be lost in thought. As soon as he sees me, he pulls himself together and kneels in front of where I sit on the couch.

"Hey, gorgeous."

"Hi."

"How are you holding up?"

I stop to think about how to answer that, "Umm, could be better...I think I'm going to take Lizzie to my parents' house and maybe stay there tonight..."

Landon nods, "That's understandable and probably a good idea. Do you still want to go out this weekend? I would be perfectly okay if you wanted to reschedule."

My answer is swift and sure. "No. I'm very much looking forward to Saturday."

He smiles, "I'm looking forward to it too, baby girl." His smile falls a little. "Do you want me to take the two of you to your parents' house? I'm more than happy to do it."

I'm already shaking my head, "We'll be okay."

He doesn't look convinced, so I lean close to his ear, cup his jaw, and whisper, "I promise, Daddy, we'll be okay."

When he pulls back, his eyes are heated and he nods his head as his hands slide up my thighs and squeeze tight before he stands.

***

SATURDAY NIGHT

The girls are over to help me get dressed for this date, since I have no idea where we're going. Landon told me to wear whatever I wanted when I asked for the dress code, so I have absolutely nothing to go on to pick out an outfit. My room is trashed, my parents are on their way to pick up Lizzie, and Landon will be here in...thirty minutes to pick me up. *Great.*

"Guys, I have to pick an outfit. I still have to do my makeup, and I'm out of time to even attempt to do anything with my hair." We're surrounded by every dress and blouse I own, and I hate everything. This is what I get for not keeping up with my wardrobe. It's easily been four years since I bought anything that could be passably "nice".

Ginny and Katy are both utterly exasperated by my indecision, and based on the looks on their faces, are completely done with my shit.

"Listen, babe. Everything here can be dressed up or down to fit most situations. You're overthinking all of it."

"Katy is right, lovey. You have something to wear; you're just in your own head. It's time to take the leap...Matt wouldn't want you to close yourself off to the possibility of loving someone else."

Bless it. They're right, I know they are, but this is terrifying.

Ugh! Okay. Time to put my big-girl panties on.

I can do this, I can do this, I can do this.

With that playing on repeat, I grab a forest green top, the black bell-bottoms, and my wedges, hoping that this will be okay for whatever we're doing tonight.

I've just finished adding my lipstick, a shade I affectionately call "fuck-me red", when I hear the doorbell ring. The girls are in the living room with Lizzie, so I take my time fluffing my hair and heading to the door. I stop mid-step, halfway down the hall, when I hear Landon's voice talking...to my parents.

I slowly come around the corner and pause to take in the scene. My parents are talking to Landon, Ginny, and Katy, while Lizzie plays on the floor...in Landon's lap. Because, of course, this completely gorgeous man is on the floor with my daughter, playing with her and her baby dolls as if it's a normal thing. Everyone seems to be having a good time together as they chat and lounge around my living room. I can't help but feel a sense of rightness at the scene laid out before me. Like everything is settled for the first time in a while.

Maybe us being together wouldn't be so bad after all.

Landon notices me first, and to say that I don't relish the way his eyes darken and the dimple peeks out on his cheek as he smiles would be an outright lie. He leans down to whisper something in Lizzie's ear, and then she's barreling toward me full tilt. She slams into my legs, looks up, and says "Mama pwetty!" before returning to her spot on the floor, where my mom has taken up residence to allow Landon to stand.

"You look breathtaking, Hope." He leans in to kiss my cheek and whispers, "Good enough to eat," in my ear before he pulls back with a Cheshire grin on his face. I can't help the blush that steals over my face at the compliments. I force out a choked "Thank you," while I try to get myself under control.

My dad steps up to give me a hug and a hello before telling me he thinks I look beautiful. Turning, he looks at Landon with his sternest glare. "Just where do you plan on taking my little girl tonight?"

Landon doesn't miss a beat. Keeping a hand on the small of my back, he looks my father in the eye as he answers. "Nowhere super exciting. If it's okay with her, I was going to take her to my place to cook for her. If not, I have a reservation at my favorite Italian restaurant. The choice is completely up to her; I'm prepared for either one."

All eyes turn to me, and I freeze, slightly panicking at having to make the choice right here in front of everyone. *I hate making decisions like this.* Landon must feel my tension winding tighter because he looks at me and says, "There's no rush, baby. We don't have to decide right this second. I'm here early. I wanted to try to spend some time with you and Lizzie both, on the off chance she was still here." Hearing that he wanted to spend time with my daughter just as much as with me brings tears to my eyes. *This man can't be real.* I poke him in the cheek just to be sure.

Huffing a laugh, he gently takes my hand, "What was that for?"

I shrug my shoulders. "Just checking to make sure you're real and not a vivid hallucination." Landon starts to lean into me, dropping his head for a sinful kiss if the look in his eyes is anything to go by, when a throat clears. *Oops! Forgot we have company.* Landon doesn't seem the least bit phased by the intense moment, which is only mildly annoying since I, again, have a furious blush stealing over my face.

Ginny and Katy make the rounds, saying goodbye, as they head to the door. My parents follow suit, with Lizzie in tow, shortly after.

Kneeling down to give Lizzie a hug and kiss, I tell her, "Be good for Lolli and Pops, okay? I love you, my sweet girl."

She lays a wet kiss on my cheek with a sweet, "Otay mama! Love you!"

And then there were two…

Once we're alone, Landon doesn't hide how his eyes rake over my body. My body has a visceral reaction to his caress-like perusal. When he's taken his fill, he looks back in my eyes, "You, baby girl, look utterly ravishing. And like you're ready to be ravished."

I stand there for what feels like an eternity, trying to process his words and form a response. The best I can manage is a squeaked-out "Thanks." Taking a minute to compose myself, I get my first true look at Landon.

Holy hot damn, sweet baby Jesus!

He looks delicious in his dark-wash denim and white button-down. He cuffed the sleeves at his elbows, so I'm getting some grade A forearm porn as I take my turn eyeing him over. The way the definition of his chest fills out the shirt is mouthwatering; you can tell he's built without it looking like he's wearing a shirt that's two sizes too small. And his jeans? The way the fabric clings to his form makes me jealous. It looks like it's giving him a firm hug. When I've finally finished eye-fucking him, I look back up into his smiling face.

With a wink, he says, "If you're done, I'd love to actually take you out. I'm afraid we won't be leaving if we stay here much longer, with you dressed like that and giving me that look."

I can't bite back my grin, "Oh I'm nowhere near done, but I am hungry. So maybe you should feed me before my evil twin makes an appearance."

He huffs a laugh while I burst into a fit of giggles at my terrible joke. Composing myself once more, we make our way to the door, chatting idly about mundane things all the way to the car: the weather, what we did today, and our favorite music. He opens the door to his Chevrolet and helps me in, making sure I'm buckled before closing the door and rounding the hood to get in himself. Once he's settled and the engine is running he turns to me and asks, "Where to? My place or the restaurant?"

I had thought my nerves were settled thanks to our easy banter, but nope! Here they are again, making my stomach flutter. I really want to go out together, see how he interacts with the staff of the restaurant; I believe you can tell a lot about a person by the way they treat those in the service industry. I also really want to see his place, how he keeps his home, and test how good of a chef he is. I must take too long because Landon grabs my hand, threads our fingers together, and traces circles along the back of my thumb.

"Hey, if you want to stay here, we can. If you want to go somewhere else, we can do that too. There's absolutely no pressure here. I only want to spend the evening with you, in whatever way you're comfortable with."

Cue the swoon! Can he be any more perfect?!

"I'm okay, I promise. It's just been a while since I've done the whole 'first date' thing." Taking a steadying breath, I bite the bullet and make a decision. "Let's do dinner out, I don't care where. After that, let's see where the night takes us."

Landon gives me a soft smile, kisses my knuckles, and throws the truck in reverse. "Sounds like a plan, baby girl. Let's go."

As we pull out of the driveway, I take in the quiet street. Couples are out walking and enjoying the evening air. I look over and notice a car on the street I've never seen before. I only noticed because of the pretty sunflower rearview mirror decoration hanging down. *I love sunflowers.* It definitely wasn't there earlier this afternoon when I ran errands, but I brush it off. *It's probably someone here visiting a neighbor.*

The drive is pleasant, filled with light small talk

interspersed with comfortable silences. Landon has his right hand on my thigh the entire time, absentmindedly rubbing his thumb back and forth as he drives one-handed. *Am I the only one who thinks it's at least a little bit sexy when a guy takes a turn one-handed because he doesn't want to take his other hand back?*

We pull up to the restaurant in what seems like no time at all. Parking in the city isn't the easiest thing to do, but Landon does it quickly and flawlessly. The hostess gives Landon a quick once-over when he walks up to give his name, and a spark of recognition flares in her eyes that is quickly followed by lust. She hardly spares me a second glance as she openly flirts with him while walking us to our table, but Landon doesn't seem to notice, his hand placed firmly at the small of my back. With a huff, the hostess finally leaves us to our evening.

The interior of the restaurant is lovely with a large chandelier hanging in the center of the ceiling above tables draped in white tablecloths. There's a large area rug covering the majority of the dining room with round tables spread throughout the space. There's a tea light candle in the center of the table and neatly folded napkins set in front of our chairs. It feels so intimate with the dimmed lighting and our small setup in the corner of the room. Picking up the menu, I start my perusal of entree items.

"See anything you like?"

I arch my brow and give him a pointed look over my menu making him huff a laugh in response. "On the menu, brat. Do you see anything you'd like to eat off the menu?"

"I'll probably get the mushroom ravioli. What about you?"

"I think I'll try something new and get the chicken francese. Sounds pretty good."

I glance over everything in the dish and suddenly feel like

I should try something different. My eyes bounce back and forth between the choices, overwhelmed by options.

"I'll give you a bite of mine if you give me a bite of yours," he offers with a smile. I guess I don't hide my sudden indecision very well.

I take him up on the offer with a relieved smile, "Deal!"

***

Dinner goes by in the blink of an eye, and soon enough, the check is being dropped off by another waiter, but we don't really pause our conversation long enough to see who it was. We offer up a quick thanks to him as he walks away. As Landon looks down at the bill, his smile drops a fraction. I wouldn't have even noticed if I hadn't been paying attention.

"Is something wrong?"

He glances back up at me, forcing his smile back in place, "Not at all. Just something I need to have a chat with the manager about."

"Is the bill incorrect? I'm sure we can just ask the waiter to fix it without dragging his boss into it."

"No, baby girl. It's not incorrect, but there is something I wish to discuss with the manager."

What the hell is going on?

I look down to see what it could be, but Landon has the check covered with his card already. I quickly reach across the table to snatch the bill from him while he's distracted, waving down the waiter. What I see makes my face flush hot in embarrassment.

Landon tries to talk to me, but I can't hear him over the roaring in my ears. I don't think I'll ever be able to unsee what's written. *"Call me when you're done with little Miss Piggy ;)"*

Who the fuck does something like this?!

I can't be here anymore.

I need to get out. Now.

I'll call an Uber and wait at the hotel down the street.

I'm halfway out of my chair before I realize that Landon is kneeling in front of me, hands on my thighs, squeezing, trying to pull me out of my head. I look down at him and feel the first tear slide down my cheek. He reaches up to wipe it away with his thumb just as the manager comes over with a glass of ice water.

He looks so concerned.

That's when I notice the silence. The hum of people talking is gone, no more silverware clattering against plates, hardly any shuffling noises from walking across the rug. Nothing. Everyone is staring at me.

I look back at Landon and whisper, "Get me out of here."

That's all it takes. Before I know it, his jacket is wrapped around my shoulders and he's whisking me away from the scene of my embarrassing panic spiral. We walk past the hostess and she gives a cheery "Come back soon," to Landon before giving me a hateful smirk.

She's the one who wrote that awful message?

I stop mid-step, causing Landon, and apparently the manager, to bump into me. I turn to look fully at the hostess, taking her in. She's one of those supermodel, skinny types. The kind of woman who has no issue finding jeans that fit perfectly in the waist, thighs, and ass. Her hair is a glossy black, full of volume and soft waves. Stepping closer, I lean in so she can hear me clearly.

"How dare you. What the actual fuck is wrong with you?! You not only blatantly disrespected me by giving your number to my date, but you had the gall to tear me down while doing it. Be warned: you reap what you sow, bitch."

With that, I turn and walk out. There's no reason to linger to see if she has a response; she already got the reaction she wanted from me. I sure as hell won't stay to explain my life to a shallow bitch like her. And I won't give her the satisfaction of watching me continue to fall apart.

I look back when I hear Landon's outraged voice, "...I don't give a fuck who she thinks she is, I want her fired. I will personally see to it that every client I have is informed of her character— "

I cut him off mid-rant, "Landon! It's fine. It's done and over and I just want to leave. I've had enough humiliation for one night."

He turns his furious eyes to me and suddenly I wish I hadn't spoken. "I will *not* have my girl treated like that, *ever*," he says in a dangerous, flat tone. "And we will discuss your disregard on the matter when we get home."

I really shouldn't have spoken.

He turns that icy stare back to the manager who shrinks back a bit at the intensity behind his eyes. The poor man looks like he's going to pee himself. "O-of course, sir. I wanted to speak with the lady before you both left anyway. My waiter informed me that she had lost some color in her face and looked ill. Which is why I came to the table." He turns apologetic eyes to me and Landon pulls me into his side, "I am sincerely sorry for the treatment you've received here tonight. I can assure you she won't be here should you ever come back. I don't tolerate that sort of behavior in anyone — not in my personal or professional life."

"Thank you for the apology, but I don't think it's fair for her to lose out on her job completely."

Landon's arm tightens around me, and before he can interject, the manager says, "She was on thin ice as it is. I won't go into details, but even if she weren't I would still let her go. As I mentioned before, I don't tolerate that type of behavior."

Landon pulls me toward the parking lot and hustles me into the car. After he pulls the seatbelt across, he grabs my chin with his thumb and index finger, turning my face toward his when he tells me, "This discussion is far from over," before he stamps a quick, claiming kiss on my mouth and slams the car door.

Fuck.

I wait for Landon to get in the car, staring out the windshield and watching him round the car when something across the lot catches my attention. *Funny, it kinda looks like the car from the neighbor's house.* I shake the thought off. It's not like there's only one person in the world who drives that make and model. Besides, I can't tell if there's a sunflower rearview mirror hanging ornament. The drive home is silent, and not exactly the pleasant kind. I try a few times to speak, opening and closing my mouth, not finding the right words to say. We drive for forty minutes before he turns off the interstate, but it's the wrong exit for my place. I turn to look at Landon to say something, but he beats me to it.

With a white-knuckled grip on the steering wheel and a ticking jaw, "We're going to my place for a bit. We're going to discuss why you tried to let some petty, pathetic nobody get away with disrespecting what's mine."

I have no idea how to respond to that, so I don't. I sit silently, wringing my fingers together, anxiously anticipating what's to come.

CHAPTER 10

LANDON

I'm fuming.

I can't believe she was going to just take the disrespect. I'm *pissed*! Though more at myself and that wretched woman than her. I should've just taken the bill to the bar to ask for a manager instead of trying to flag down the waiter.

And the gall of that woman! I saw she wanted me as soon as she made eye contact with me, but I only wanted to pay attention to Hope so she decided to take matters into her own hands and insult my woman in the process. As if that's any way to go about getting attention. Although, for her to have been so bold, she must've had a few takers in the past.

Whatever. None of my concern.

My concern is sitting in the passenger seat of my truck, wringing her fingers together to the point they are turning red. We'll be home soon, and I can take this in a more constructive direction.

My place comes into view within another fifteen minutes of driving. It's nothing fancy; I didn't see the need for anything monstrously huge since it's just me. This was actually one of the first houses James and I did in college. It was originally a little three-bedroom split-level, but we turned the "downstairs" into a fourth bedroom. There was something about the craftsman-style architecture that I loved. I made sure we kept it as close to the original floor plan as possible, and when we finished, I decided to keep it as my own.

As we pull up, I can see Hope's eyes take in the exterior of the house. There's a small front porch with a swing and a simple flower bed under that, filled with flowers and other plant life I couldn't name if I tried. I just pull the weeds and the blooms keep coming back each year. The landscapers we contacted when we renovated this place gave us a list of easily maintained plant-life that we could get for cheap. We just sort of picked at random and hoped for the best.

I park and get out of the car, jogging around the front to open Hope's door for her. She looks up at me hesitantly before she speaks.

"I'm sorry for the way dinner ended. Especially for the way I reacted to the note on the bill. I shouldn't have let it bother me as much as it did. It was stupid and unbecoming of a woman of my age."

"Hope, baby girl, you have absolutely nothing to apologize for. I'm more upset with myself and that hateful bitch at the restaurant than with you. I shouldn't have left it for you to see in the first place. For that, I'm the one who is sorry." I grab both sides of her head and tilt her face up to mine so she can see the sincerity on my face. "That woman was cruel, just because she didn't get what she wanted. And the fact that she was so blatant about it tells me she's done it before and had some degree of success. What I want to focus on is your reaction to what she wrote. Come inside. I want to talk."

She nods her head, looking rather dejected about the coming conversation. We walk silently through the garage and into the house. There's a closed and locked door straight ahead that I hope to show her soon, but for now, I take her up the few stairs and into the main living space. I kept the color palette fairly neutral with grey tones and navy blue accents; something warm and inviting yet calming. It's an open concept in the main rooms, with a large sectional couch to create dimension in the living room, and an old, oak kitchen table I found at an antique store. The kitchen has all stainless-steel appliances with a sealed concrete countertop. Stopping in the entryway by the front door, I turn her to face me.

"Hope, I'm going to punish you. Pick a safeword, baby. If at any point you want to stop, say it, and everything stops. No questions asked. If you stop, I will ask you what prompted you to do so, and I want you to be completely honest in your answer. Nothing half-assed. Do I make myself clear?"

She looks completely dumbfounded before she starts spluttering, "P-punish me? What the fuck are you talking about?!"

I stare at her for a minute, letting the shock wear off and realization dawn on her. When her face goes slack as her mind catches up, I continue.

"Tonight, you believed the vitriol spewed at you instead of remembering who you are and how much beauty you carry inside and out. I could see it written all over your face. Why?"

"Because it's true. I am chunky. I never lost all the baby weight, and my weight fluctuated a lot before getting pregnant. She shouldn't have said anything, because who the fuck says that about someone?! But she also didn't say anything untrue."

When she finishes speaking, I can feel my blood pressure climbing and hear it roaring in my ears. *She can't honestly believe any of this.* But I see it in her expression and her closed-off body language; she really believes every word that just came out of her mouth. I take a deep breath to calm and center myself before I continue.

"You're mine now, Hope. We are going to work on your self-perception together, starting tonight. Will you trust me with this? There won't be any physical pain, though I won't promise you won't cry. That's entirely up to you."

"What do you mean there won't be physical pain? What are you expecting me to do?"

"Pick your safeword and I'll explain what will happen after that."

She seems a little lost, her eyes furiously bouncing around the room as she tries to think of something.

"Take a deep breath, baby. It can be any word you want, as long as it's not something you would normally say in a conversation or the heat of the moment."

Nodding, she takes a breath and closes her eyes as she focuses on calming herself.

"Red."

"Good girl. When you use that, everything stops. Do you understand?"

"I understand."

I place a quick kiss on her forehead. "Good girl. You're going to spend half an hour in time-out. I will give you a dry-erase marker, and you will stand naked in front of the mirror, alone, writing the things you like and dislike about yourself. After that time, I will join you and write what I love about you."

I watch her eyes widen as I explain the punishment. Her fear of this is practically tangible, and while I want her to think about how she perceives herself, this is not designed to instill fear.

"Landon, I can't tell you how much I don't want to do that.

I don't even look at myself below the shoulders when I'm out of the shower. I can't."

Her voice starts to wobble. I want to comfort her, but I can't yet. I want to drive my point home. I need her to know how beautiful she is; to me and all the people around her. I step closer to her, just a fraction, and ask her again.

"Will you trust me with this? I swear to you, if you need to use the safeword there will be no questions or consequences. We will stop. I'll wait in the bedroom with one of my t-shirts for you to put on if you need it, but I really think this will be good for you." I wait with baited breath to see what she'll decide.

God, I hope she does. I think she needs this, that it could be good for her.

Slowly, *oh so slowly*, she nods her head, and my heart rate soars.

"Words, Hope. Use your words or I will spank that pert, little ass until you can't sit tomorrow." My voice drops to a lower register, speaking the words aloud, from both anticipation of what's to come and the arousal starting to bleed into my system at her agreement.

"I'll agree to try it as long as you're serious about the safeword. If I say it, I can stop? You won't get upset?"

"I'm serious, baby girl. You say it, everything stops, and I won't get upset. I'll be more upset if you don't use it despite needing to."

She relents with a sigh. "Okay. Where am I going?"

I grab her hand and bring her through my bedroom to my bathroom. The color scheme continues with the neutral palette in here, but just a shade darker to help me unwind at the end of the day. The shower curtain, bathmat, and rug are navy blue;

so dark they look almost black. I have an over-the-door mirror hanging on my closet door at the back of the space, which is where I bring Hope now. We completely bypass the oversized soaking tub, the double-head shower stall, and the double vanity set in a white engineered stone countertop over dark-stained cabinets. Stopping in front of the mirror, I pull Hope in front of me, "Wait here, baby girl."

She gives me a weak, "Okay." I stride quickly from the bathroom and head to the office across the hall from my bedroom, where I grab two dry-erase markers off the whiteboard. I come back to the bathroom to find Hope right where I left her, staring blankly into the mirror. I really hate the sad, scared look on her face. As I approach her, I uncap one of the markers and draw an upside-down T-chart on the mirror, explaining as I go.

"The left side is for what you like about yourself, the right is for your dislikes. Under this bottom line is space for me to write what I love about you. Any questions?"

"No."

"From now on, I want you to address me as Daddy. Alright?"

She hesitates for a split second, "Okay...Daddy."

Hearing her call me that? It might be my new favorite thing, ever.

Would it be weird to ask her if I can record her saying it? Definitely. Definitely weird. Don't ask her that.

Focusing back on the task at hand, I lean into her so she can feel the effect she has on me and order, "Strip, baby girl. Show me what's mine."

She takes a few steadying breaths before bending over to

undo the straps on her shoes. She kicks them aside and starts to undo the button of her pants, the ones that look damn near painted on, the ones I've been fantasizing about taking off all fucking night, and now I can't because she's in time-out.

I should've thought this through.

As she bends to pull her pants over her hips, she has to do a little shimmy, and I can't bite back my groan at the sight before me. She pauses with her pants halfway down her thighs and straightens to look back at me with a cocked brow and a pointed glance at my quickly tenting pants.

"Keep going, baby girl," I all but growl at her. She reaches for her panties next, and I can't stop the words that come tumbling out of my mouth. "No. Leave them. If you take them off, I can't guarantee I'll continue to be good."

She smirks at me with a hopeful gleam in her eyes, "Would that really be so bad?"

"Hope, if you take those panties off, I will grab you by the hair, push you into that mirror, and make you watch me turn your ass a bright red before I fuck you. That is not the goal here. Keep the panties on. Be a good girl, and I promise, I will make it worthwhile."

I can see her contemplating the consequences of taking the panties off. Thankfully, she must see the unhinged look in my eyes because she moves on to her top, swiftly pulling it up and over her head. When she moves for her bra, I have to clench my hands into fists to stop myself from reaching out.

There's going to be scars left on my palms at this rate.

She looks back at me, seemingly to see if I want her to remove it, so I give her a slight nod and watch her unsnap the clasp. There's a brief look of complete bliss when it comes off that makes me a little mad that I didn't put it there myself, but

I lose all rational thought when her tits bounce free of their confinement.

Oh fuck, *I'm in trouble.*

My voice is pure grit when I speak again. "Okay, Hope. Time starts now. You have thirty minutes to write as much as you can about yourself; your likes and dislikes. If you run out of things to say, you'll continue to stand there until time is up. Do you understand?"

"Yes, Daddy. I understand."

Internally groaning, I turn to leave her to it.

"Good girl. Get started."

"Wait..."

"What is it, baby girl?"

"Will you stay? I'll just stand here if you walk out."

I contemplate it, thinking of a way to walk out of here so I don't cave and take her right here and now.

"Please..." she whispers.

Steeling myself, I take a deep breath and agree to stay. She relaxes a touch and looks back at herself in the mirror as I lean against the vanity. While I'm currently battling a raging hard on, the likes of which I've never felt before, I'm proud of her for speaking up and being honest about what she needs from me at this moment.

She spends a few minutes looking at herself, starting with her face. In the Likes column, she writes things like "hair, smile, eyes," but as she moves down her body, more and more starts to go on the other side of the line. She puts things like "saggy boobs, stretch marks, mom-apron, waistline," and it breaks my heart to see the right side get longer as she goes on, "freckles, dimples on my ass, flabby arms."

When she's finally done writing, fifteen minutes have passed. Tears are slowly making their way down her cheeks, and she angrily wipes them away.

"You're doing so well, baby girl. You have fifteen minutes left. Write anything else that comes to mind."

She nods and whispers, "Okay, Daddy," as she continues to stand there and stare at her reflection.

Time ticks down slowly in the last ten minutes, and I use that time to look her over. Comparing her thoughts to mine. I look at her list again and start making up my own. Walking forward, I let my body graze hers for the first time since we got home. I love the way she leans into me, like she needs me for support right now. Reaching around, I take the marker and start my list, reading each item off as I go.

"Your hair, I love how it moves with you and how you've cut it. It suits you. Your eyes are the most beautiful shade of blue I've ever seen; I especially love the ring of green around the pupil. The smile lines around your eyes, that's actually one of the first things I noticed about you. You could tell that you love to smile and do it often enough to leave a permanent reminder of how incredible it is. Your mouth; I love the shape, the color, the fullness...everything; I love how long your neck is, it gives me plenty of room to lean in like this and lick..." I give a slow, languorous slide of my tongue. "Kiss..." I say as I pepper kisses down the long column of her throat. "Suck..." *It's probably childish of me to hope I leave a hickey, but I do all the same.* "...and nibble as I please..." I pause to do just that, taking my time and enjoying the taste of her skin before I continue.

"I love your tits, another thing I noticed about you the night we met. I thought 'damn, they look like the perfect amount to squeeze and have just a little left over' and when I learned you had a kid? Lord forgive me for the mental image of these tits leaking milk to provide for that baby that flashed through my head. And this tummy? Oh, baby. This stomach provided shelter for that beautiful little girl of yours. Imagining you pregnant and glowing is so fucking sexy to me. Those stretch marks you say you don't like? I love them. They show everyone how fucking fierce you are to have put your body through what it takes to grow another human. Your waistline is probably my favorite though. I love this little dip right here above your hips. It's like a neon sign saying 'grip here for fun'."

We both giggle at that, though hers is a little watery.

"Baby girl, everything about you is beautiful, and the people in this world that are hell-bent on tearing you down do so out of envy. They're jealous of your light, of the joy you give the people around you, because they know they don't have it and will never get it without first working on themselves. Don't ever let someone try to dim your light again. You. Are. Mine." I hold her chin as I tilt her head a little higher. "And my girl will walk with her head held high and that incredible smile on her face, knowing that her light makes my world shine brighter just for knowing her."

By the time I'm done speaking, she is openly crying. I turn her to face me and hold her tightly. "You did so well, baby girl. I'm so fucking proud of you. I know you didn't want to do this. I could see how much you hated it, but you followed through. Such a good girl." I give her a minute to settle and process everything we've just done before telling her, "Tell me what you've learned from this."

She takes a full minute to calm herself before she answers, sniffling as she does, "I learned I need to be kinder to myself. That I need to give myself some grace because of all the things my body has gone through, and I need to remember that it will take time and effort to change anything that I want to improve."

"That's right, my sweet girl. Time and effort, give grace, and be kind. Aren't those all things you would expect from Lizzie? Why wouldn't you expect the same of yourself?" I bring her to the counter and sit her down next to the sink, "I'm going to wipe your face with a cool rag, give you a t-shirt to put on, and then we're going to snuggle in bed with a bowl of ice cream and berries while we watch a movie. Sound like a plan?"

I get the sweetest smile from my girl when she gives me a sleepy, "Yes, Daddy. That sounds wonderful."

I'm done for.

I leave Hope in my room as I head to the kitchen to make all the snacks I promised before I head back to join her. When I get back, she's snuggled under the blankets with the TV remote in hand, surfing through Netflix to find something to watch. I can't help but fantasize about this being a regular, everyday thing. Her in my bed, wearing my shirt, waiting for me to come back to her with snacks so we can cuddle after a long day at the office. Lizzie will be down the hall in a room just for her, sleeping soundly while Hope and I...

I have to stop that thought in its tracks before I get carried away...although...I don't hate the idea of making space for Lizzie soon. I want to show Hope how serious I am about us, that I understand that she's a package deal.

I'll start looking at designs Monday morning.

I crawl into bed next to Hope while she puts on The Great British Bake-Off and holds out her hands to take her bowl of ice cream and berries. We stay like that for a long time. With each episode that passes, Hope moves a little bit closer. By the third episode, I have my arm thrown around her, and her head rests on my chest. I think she's fallen asleep until her right hand starts sliding across my abdomen, fingers angled toward the waistband of the sweats I threw on in the bathroom before I joined her in bed.

"What are you doing, baby girl?"

She lets out the cutest giggle, and her voice holds the haze of exhaustion in its rasp when she replies, "I thought that was obvious, Daddy."

I catch her wrist right as her fingertips dip below the band.

"Little girl, don't start something you're too tired to finish."

"I'm not tired, Daddy! Promise." She says around a jaw-popping yawn.

"Don't lie to Daddy, little girl. You'll get a spanking this time, and you're not ready for that yet."

Her body tenses for a second before she looks up at me, eyes clouded with exhaustion and lust.

Fuck.

"You like that idea, don't you, baby?"

"I do, Daddy. Please let me touch you. I want to feel your cock."

Groaning, "Hope. Baby. Don't say something like that. I'm begging you."

She has an evil grin on her face when she looks me dead in the eye and starts begging.

"Please, Daddy? Please let me feel your cock. I want to slide my hands over it, taste you on my tongue..."

Before she can continue, I roll her over and pull up the t-shirt she put on after her time-out to expose her panties.

Raking my gaze over the exposed flesh, "Are you clean? On birth control?"

"I'm clean. I haven't been with anyone since Matt, and I'm on the pill."

"Perfect." I take a moment to admire her black lace cheeky panties before I dip my fingers inside, searching. I can't help the moan that comes from my throat when I feel how wet she is.

"Is this for me, baby girl? How long have you been like this?"

Panting as my fingers glide through her slick heat, "Since we got in bed. I don't know why I'm wet from the punishment; it made me cry. I shouldn't be wet, but I am." She throws her head back in a moan as I sink one finger inside her heated core.

"Oh! Don't stop. Please. Please don't stop. So good."

"You started this, baby, but I'm ending it."

She looks adorably confused when I pull my finger back out. My grin is shit-eating when I tell her what she's gotten herself into.

"You'll get to come, don't worry about that. But you're going to beg me for it before you do." With that, I pop the finger that was inside her into my mouth and close my eyes as I savor her taste.

When I open them again, Hope's eyes are so dark she looks possessed. I bring one hand to her neck and slide the other back to her panties. When I slide my finger back inside her, I give her neck a firm but gentle squeeze, gauging her reaction. My grip isn't enough to restrict airflow, but just to hold her still and remind her who is in control. Judging by the flutter in her pussy,

I'd say she likes it, so I keep my hand on her throat while I start to move my finger inside her.

I pull it out, to slide up to her clit, stroking it until I feel her pulse accelerate under the hand around her throat. When her eyes close and her breathing changes, I stop. Her eyes fly wide and land on me with murder in them. I can't help but laugh as I start all over again. Lightly rubbing her clit before sliding down to her entrance and pushing in with one finger. I work in a "come here" motion, feeling her walls tighten ever so slightly as she starts to climb higher again. Just before she falls over the cliff, I stop again. This time, she yells.

"Landon! What the fuck?!"

"I told you, baby girl. You're going to beg. We can do this all night. And if you use my name again before you come, I'm going to spank this pussy until you come that way instead of just using my gentle fingers. Understood?"

Her gulp is audible, "Yes, Daddy. I'm sorry."

I kiss her nose and squeeze her throat lightly, relishing in her groan when I do.

"Good girl."

With that, I continue my torturous teasing. Endlessly bringing her to the edge over and over before stopping. It takes longer than I thought it would. By the time Hope is begging through her tears, Netflix has stopped playing in the background, but she's finally begging.

Tears stream down her face as she pleads, "Please, Daddy. P-please. D-don't stop. Make me come. Please!"

With a smile planted firmly on my face, I stuff her pussy with two fingers and push on her clit with my thumb. The pressure combined with the movement of my fingers inside her soaked pussy sends her flying. She releases a scream of pleasure and her body shakes as she flies over the edge. I continue rubbing her through it all, until she feebly tries to push my hand away.

Scooping her into my side, I settle us under the covers again before pushing play on Netflix. Hope's breathing is ragged, but settling the longer we lie there. I turn my head to kiss the top of her head, whispering, "Good fucking girl."

I can feel her grin as she sleepily says, "Thank you, Daddy."

It's not long after that we both fall asleep.

CHAPTER 11
Landon

I wake to someone pounding on my door.

Hope groans and rolls over onto her stomach. I don't want the incessant pounding to wake her, so I quickly throw on a pair of sweatpants and race to the door. I have no idea what time it is, but it's still dark, which means it's entirely too early for anyone to be awake. I fling it open, ready to lay into whoever is on the other side only to find my doorstep empty and a box sitting on my welcome mat.

I do not *want to open that, not after the box that was sent to Hope's house.*

I can't leave this on my porch, and I won't leave it for Hope to find in the house in the morning. I release a resigned sigh and bend to pick it up when something catches my eye. I look to my left and see someone standing under the streetlight up the road. Whoever it is, she's definitely a woman, but that's the only thing I can discern. She's too far to make out any details.

"Nope!" I quickly stand, close and lock the door, and take a great gasping breath when I have the door between me and the crazy person up the road. I hear Hope's sleepy voice call for me from the stairs and turn to see her standing there trying to rub the sleep from her eyes.

Fuck, she's so damn cute like this.

"Hey, baby girl. Is everything okay?"

"Yeah, I rolled over and didn't feel you." She pauses and looks me over, "Are *you* okay?"

I contemplate telling Hope about the box, but I really want her to rest so I decide to wait until morning.

"I'm fine, baby."

I must not look convincing, though, because she asks if I'm sure.

"Yeah, nothing that can't wait until morning."

I go back to bed with Hope and dread the coming morning. I don't want to tell her–I really don't–but I won't lie to her.

I wake up before Hope the next morning, and I quietly head down the stairs and to the front door. I hesitate for a moment, not wanting to open the door, but I take a breath and do it anyway. The box isn't there anymore, but there is an envelope. I look up and down the street, but don't see anyone, so I bend to pick it up. It's addressed to me. I open the flap as I turn back into the house.

You didn't like my gift?

I'm sorry. I'll stick to flowers for now.

I hope you liked the last rose!

I'm not too macho to admit my hands are shaking as I stare at the note. I'm so lost in my head that I don't hear Hope come up behind me until her hands snake around my waist, making me jump.

She burrows into my back, "Thanks for letting me sleep, Daddy."

"Uh-huh. No problem, baby girl."

She tenses a little at my tone and comes around to my front. She sees the note in my hands and asks, "Do I want to read that?"

I shake my head, "Probably not. It seems you're not the only one receiving unwanted gifts."

Hope burrows into my chest, and I secure my arms around her shoulders, "What is happening, Landon?"

I lean over and kiss her head, "I have no idea, baby girl."

She huddles in closer to me, arms wrapped tight around my waist. I gently pull her back toward the kitchen and sit her down at the table. Kneeling in front of her, I take her hands in mine.

"I wish this wasn't happening, but it is. That being said, I'm going to do everything in my power to figure it out."

She doesn't answer right away, taking me in. Slowly, she nods. "I believe you. Not entirely sure what you can do, but I believe you when you say you'll try."

I place my forehead on her lap and huff out a laugh, "Honesty, I'm not sure either. I'll figure it out though." She starts running her fingers through my hair, letting her nails scrape against the back of my neck. There's nothing I can do to stop the groan that tumbles out as I burrow further into her lap, nuzzling her delicious thighs and breathing in her scent.

"Fuck that feels so good." She lets out the sweetest little giggle, and I resolve myself to hear it more often. Sighing, I reluctantly push up to my feet and head to the kitchen. "Okay, baby girl, enough of that or you won't get any of my famous pancakes. I need to feed you before I drag you back to bed and don't let you out for the rest of the day."

She gives me another giggle as she sidles up next to me and leans in. "Whatever you say, Daddy."

Fuck, I love the way that sounds.

CHAPTER 12

Hope

ONE MONTH LATER

The last month with Landon has been great. Our first date started off wonderfully. Aside from the hateful woman trying to interfere, the evening was actually quite nice...punishment included. While it certainly wasn't fun, it gave me perspective. It reminded me that I need to give myself some grace. I don't have to be perfect, just happy and healthy for myself and my daughter. The next morning, however, was scary. The note wasn't threatening, but it was unnerving. The fact that someone delivered a package, took it back, and then left a note on his front porch is terrifying.

Who the hell could this be? Who delivered the snout to my house?

Date number two went much better. He took me for brunch at a cute little place with these outrageously large flower displays hanging from the ceiling. I had been wanting to visit but never thought I actually would. The food was okay, but I was more there for the company and the atmosphere than anything else.

Work is great too.

My parents have been amazing, helping me out by watching Lizzie where they can. On the days that they can't, I send her to a cute little preschool, or I give my in-laws a call. When the school is closed and no one else is available, I work from home. I hate feeling like a burden to everyone, but I've made every accommodation I can while still working.

There hasn't been anything too difficult in all honesty, and if I hadn't already laid into both James and Landon about not taking it easy on me, I would accuse them of doing just that. Turns out, I'm overqualified for this job. After looking over the paperwork, I raised a little hell with Landon when I saw how much they were offering me. He, very calmly, informed me that he and James had discussed giving me a greater than average workload for a secretary due to my skill level, which was fine with me. I don't want to be bored at work. After my little outburst, he tied my hands to the headboard and denied me an orgasm for two hours. *Lesson learned.*

The guys have been steadily increasing my responsibilities by giving me tasks to alleviate some of Diana's workload. Three times a week, she and I split applications between ourselves and start weeding. From there, she gives me her top picks and I conduct a phone interview with the applicants before passing along the best candidates for Diana to interview in person.

Once reality sank in that I would be working with my boyfriend, I got worried that we would be spending too much time together, that we would get tired of each other, but that hasn't been the case. We compartmentalize well, actually. We have lunch together most days, although we spend more time getting intimately familiar with each other than eating. We never go past any heavy petting, though, and I'm starting to get restless. At the end of the day, he walks me to my car, gives me a kiss full of beautifully dark promises, and sends me on my way.

Landon has made it a point to include Lizzie in almost everything we do together. He's amazing with her, and she's really taken a shine to him. Sometimes, they even forget I'm in the room. It's honestly great, that little reprieve. I love what they have together. He asked me if it was okay for him to start buying toys and clothes for her to have at his house, and when I wondered why she would need something like that, he simply shrugged, "What if we have a messy date or she has an accident? I want her to be comfortable. Besides, it wouldn't hurt to have a few things at my place in case you leave after her bedtime one night."

My heart stuttered, then took off at a full gallop, hearing those words. His consideration of Lizzie, making plans that include her, sends me over the moon with joy. I'm ready to move things along. I want him to spend the night. To touch me. I want to see him naked, standing before me in all his tanned glory. Ready to make good on all the promises he made at the beginning. I want to wake up in his arms, lazing around together until Lizzie wakes up for the day.

One problem. I don't have the first clue as to how to bring it up to him. I suppose I could try just talking to him...or I could have a little fun and try my hand at seduction.

Yeah, I like that idea. Let's hope he doesn't shut me down.

I pull up Landon's number and send out a text.

Me: Sleepover at my place this weekend?

I don't even have a chance to put my phone down before his response comes through.

Landon: Yes.

Me: Goodie ;) Come over Friday after work.

Me: Think you could stay all weekend?

Landon: Try to stop me, baby girl.

Me: Can't wait! Lizzie will be at home with us, but once she goes down for the night, we'll have some alone time. See you then!

Now to plot. I mean plan.

Immediately, I call the girls. Thankfully, they have flexible schedules. Katy owns a nail salon, and Ginny works from home, so even if she is working, she can usually chat for a few minutes.

They're both available when I call, and I jump right into it without so much as a 'hello' as soon as the call connects.

"Ladies, it's past time. I need to seduce him."

Silence. Then Katy, "Wait, you guys haven't fucked yet? It's been over a month!"

"Ignore her." Ginny says as she rolls her eyes, "What's the plan?"

I love my friends!

"No, we haven't had sex yet. No, I don't know why. And my plan is still in the pregnancy stage, I have a potential idea, but it hinges on a few things…"

About this time, I remember I hadn't told the girls about the things Landon is into in the bedroom.

Guess it's now or never. Sorry, Landon!

"Okay, listen up, 'cause I'm not repeating myself."

When they're both silent, I continue. "Landon is a Daddy Dom. He told me about it the night we met. The short version of everything is that he's looking for a partner to spoil, in every sense of the word. I looked up the kink a bit, a while back. I think it seems kinda fun. To have a chance to let go."

I pause to gauge reactions, and I think the camera froze with how still they are.

"You guys still there?"

"Yeah. Yeah, we're still here."

"Okay, cool. So, anyway. I wrote up a scene on my phone for him, but I don't want to immediately jump into it. I want to tease it out a little. I was thinking of dressing up a bit, but like, not in an obviously sexy way. More like girl-next-door on laundry day."

"Go on," they encourage.

"Well, that's about where my idea fizzles out. I don't know where to go from there. Especially since Lizzie will be home."

Katy stops me, "Hold on. Why not just start with words?"

Huh. Kinda wish I had thought of that.

"Like...?" I prod.

"I don't know, like 'Please, Daddy' or begging him, maybe? What did the research show you?"

I think back to what I read on a blog from a full-time submissive. I could probably make that work. *As long as I don't have to say it out loud...then I'll just get all awkward.*

"Okay, I think I got it. Next, is outfit, hair, makeup, and nails. Katy, you got me covered on the nails?"

"You know you didn't even have to ask. Of course I do! And I already know just what to do."

"Perfect, thanks, babe! Ginny, help me out with hair and clothes?"

"Yeah, I can be over there later tonight after Lizzie goes to bed."

"I love you, girls!"

We hang up to a chorus of "See you later" and "I love you too."

After I hang up, I pull out a pad of sticky notes and one of my pens to write a few teasing notes to stick in his office throughout the rest of the week.

Can't wait for this weekend!

I'm aching for you.

Do you want to play, Daddy?

I've been such a good girl for you.

I've been so wet thinking about your touch.

I need to taste you.

It's probably overkill, but oh well! I'm having fun with this.

***

It's time!

I'm so nervous. And excited. But mostly nervous.

I've spent the week sneaking into Landon's office while he was in meetings or out running errands to leave the notes in random places. In his desk drawer, on his computer screen, on the wet bar, and even on the bathroom mirror. I think they've been turning him on because after he finds each note, Landon tracks me down and pulls me into the nearest empty room to ravage my mouth, and each time it goes a little farther. The first time, it instigated some over-the-clothes groping. The next time, he grabbed my ass and lifted me onto his desk, and we ended up having a super intense dry-hump.

Today, the note I left had him hauling me to his office, closing the door and blinds, and bending me over his desk. He pulled my panties off, bound my wrists with them, then teased my soaking pussy until I started to drip. Then he pulled me upright, untied my bound hands, pulled my skirt back down, and sent me on my way with a pat on the ass and a dark look in his eye. I had been so ready to come; eyes closed, forehead resting on his desk, just about to fall over the edge. Instead, I spent the rest of my day dripping wet and shifting in my seat, trying to get some relief. Not to mention constantly making sure there wasn't a visible wet spot on my dark grey skirt, since he didn't give me my panties back. I'm ready to get him back for that little stunt.

I'm wearing the outfit Ginny helped me pick out: the black spanx he loved so much the first time he came over paired with a plain white t-shirt just long enough to cover my ass, knee-high black socks, and slippers.

And wouldn't you know it? I forgot that all my bras are dirty.

Oops.

My nails are done in a white color with a light shimmer on top, to set it off. It looks almost virginal. I'd be mad if it wasn't so cute. I went with just some mascara and a tinted chapstick for my makeup, deciding to keep it as minimal as possible. It helps to make this all seem coincidental, since I don't really wear a whole lot of makeup to begin with.

There's a knock at the door while I'm making dinner. I check on Lizzie in the living room, making sure she's still munching on a snack at her little table while watching Ms. Rachel on the TV, before I head to answer the door. Landon is standing on the other side, looking absolutely delicious. I love seeing him in his suit and tie every day, but casual Landon?

There's a throb in my core that wasn't there a moment ago.

Low-slung, light wash jeans that look well-worn hang from his hips. They've got a few stains on them and a few holes from years of wear and tear. He topped the look with a black short sleeve t-shirt that damn near hugs him like a second skin.

How can one man make casual look so fucking sexual?

As I finish my perusal of him, I notice him standing there, slack-jawed, staring at everything on offer tonight. I internally peacock at the heated approval glowing in his eyes.

"You wanna come in, or just stand there staring with the door open all night?" I tease with a laugh. He shakes his head as if he's physically trying to force himself to refocus on something other than my outfit. He steps through the door, leaning down to kiss me as he passes. He stands back as I close the door, inhales deeply, and groans.

"What is that smell? It smells absolutely heavenly."

I blush and try to sweep over the praise. "It's nothing. Just something I put together."

"Well, what is it?"

"It's a recipe I like making. Truthfully, it was one of Matt's favorites. I try to make it here and there as a reminder."

I blanch. *Fuck!* I didn't even think to ask if that was okay! Or if he has any allergies!

"Is that okay? I don't want to upset you. I didn't even think about it. I just had all the ingredients in the fridge. I can make something else if you prefer. Do you have any allergies? I can't believe I didn't ask. I'm usually so careful about that…"

Landon interrupts my frantic babbling with a deep and heated kiss.

"Breathe, baby girl. Take a breath with me."

Oh, I hadn't even realized I had started to hyperventilate.

"Good girl, again." He puts my hand on his chest to help sync our breaths, and I start to calm down.

"Good. Now, to answer your questions. I'm not upset, promise. I don't want you to feel like you have to hide him from me. While I'll be the first to admit, I wish you were mine first. I won't ask you to hide, make you feel guilty, or try to make you regret your past. That's all it is, the past. He will always have a place in your heart, and I'd like to think there's room in there for me, too. He's Lizzie's father, and I won't hide that from her if she were to ask me about it one day. No, I don't have any allergies; I'll eat pretty much anything. Especially if you make it. If you like to cook, then cook. Whatever your heart desires. If you need an ingredient, call me and I'll either bring it to you myself or have it delivered. I want to take care of you in whatever capacity you need."

I stand in the entryway, wrapped in Landon's arms, in complete disbelief. He's talking long-term. With me and Lizzie both. I can't help the tears that slide down my cheeks.

Landon gently wipes them away, pulls me close, and lets me gather myself. Lizzie walks in a moment later, saying and signing, "Eat more? Please?" I laugh and wipe my eyes before turning to her.

"Of course, baby. Dinner is ready. Are you ready to eat?"

She repeats, "Eat? Please?"

As I turn around to lead the way to the kitchen, I see Landon is already halfway there and grabbing Lizzie's plate to dish out food. My heart trips a little. He turns to me, smiling, kissing my cheek in passing as he walks Lizzie to her seat at the table for dinner. I have ours dished up before he gets back.

"You never did tell me what this was."

I didn't?

"Oh! It's creamy garlic chicken. Heavy cream, garlic, spinach, tomato, and chicken, along with some other spices. I like it best served over pasta, but it's good with rice too."

"It smells amazing." He pauses to give me a heated look, "I can't wait to eat."

I don't think he's referring to the food.

Lucky me!

CHAPTER 13

Landon

The first thought to run through my head is: *Damn! My girl can cook!*

The second was that dinner went well. Really well. Lizzie kept us on our toes with her antics, and it was adorable. I knew it as soon as I had them both in the same room that first time. *They're mine.*

We go through the girls' normal evening routine with a bath, songs, and snuggles before bedtime at seven thirty. I never realized how much goes into simply getting ready for bed. I swear, I'm more in awe of Hope every day.

We finally sat down on the couch with a glass of red wine and both let out a deep sigh. I turn to Hope, "You amaze me."

She jerks her head to face me and snorts a laugh, "Why? I'm nothing extraordinary. I don't think I've done anything worth being amazed about."

"Stop." My voice is a little harsher than I want for this conversation. It seems my girl has a few things to learn about accepting and believing compliments when they're given.

"You're incredible. You're a young, single mother caring for an almost three-year-old little girl who is beyond happy and fed well. You do an incredible job at work. You keep in touch with your family, you have amazing friends, and you're an amazing friend yourself. Of course, I'm amazed by you." When I finish talking, her face is a precious shade of dark pink, just bordering on red. I chuckle and pull her close, "Don't sell yourself short. Not even in your own head."

She nods in acknowledgement, and I grit my teeth. *I fucking hate the nodding.*

She seems to understand her mistake, she looks at me from under hooded eyes and whispers, "Sorry, Daddy." I choke on my swallow of wine, and my cock jumps. Once I catch my breath, I look over at her. She has a slight grin on her lips, like she did it on purpose.

"Do you understand what you'll be getting yourself into?"

"Yes, Daddy. I understand."

I close my eyes, silently praying for patience. When I open them, I ask, "And what is it you understand?"

"I understand that I want you. I want to make you as happy as you've made me. I understand that, within the confines of this part of our relationship, you're in charge. I'm okay with giving up some of my control. I trust you. I'm eager to try new things with you. I want to give this a genuine shot and see where it goes, Landon. Will you be my Daddy?"

If she has anything else to say, I don't know, nor do I care.

I have to touch her. To kiss her.

Growling, I lunge for her. "You wore this shit on purpose, didn't you?"

She nods again, a devious glint in her eye.

I forgo the warning.

She's had plenty.

With a stern expression on my face, I give her ass a spank. Nothing hard, nothing that would leave a mark. Only enough to let her know there will be more if she continues to break the only rule I've set so far. She jumps at the contact, then rolls her hips into my cock. Grinding down, we both close our eyes, basking in the sensation.

I put my hands on her hips to stop her movement, and she whimpers at the loss.

"Don't give me any lip, baby girl. I've told you before, I'm only so patient. We need to talk. Set the parameters."

She pushes out her lower lip, pouting. I pull one hand from her hip to drag my thumb across that lip. Pulling it down gently to open her mouth to me, just a little. The little temptress darts her tongue out and licks the tip of my thumb, all while looking me dead in the eye.

"Keep it up, and you'll wish you listened the first time. I'm not rushing this, that's not what a good Daddy does. We'll start slow. Ease you into everything. Now, tell me your limits."

She tries to clear the lust from her brain, "Um, well, I'm not sure other than what I think is obvious. Nothing that would leave a bruise, no...bodily fluids, that sort of thing. From our first conversation, I'm okay with—and I can't believe I'm saying this —orgasm denial, spanking, and time-out as punishment. Things of that nature. I did a little research myself and found that some baby girls have stuffed animals they seem to cling to. I read where those get taken away as a punishment, kind of like a grounding. If I had one, I'd say that's fine too, but I don't, so..." She trails off when she notices my rapid breathing.

"Keep going," it comes out as nothing more than a choked rasp.

"I think that's it. I'm not a virgin or anything, so I'm willing to try almost anything once. I'll let you know if I don't like something."

I grunt. *Fuck.*

"You really are perfect."

I dive in. No longer restraining myself. I pull her mouth back to mine and plunder. My tongue flirts with hers in a dangerous dance. She groans into my mouth, and I swallow it down like a man dying of thirst. I stand, carrying her to the hallway, tearing my mouth away long enough to grunt out, "Room."

She points toward the end of the hall while sucking on the expanse of skin just below my ear. Dragging her teeth behind as she goes. I can't help the shudder that runs through me. I finally make it to her room and have to remind myself to close the door gently so we don't wake Lizzie. Throwing her on the bed, I assess my options. Wondering where to begin my feast. Raking my gaze over her splayed form, I lock my hungry stare on her.

"Strip."

CHAPTER 14

Hope

One word.

That's all he said.

But that one word held so much promise, it forced a shiver down my spine. I sat up on the bed, lifting my arms to remove my shirt. His quick inhale letting me know he's watching my every move, and that he noticed I haven't been wearing a bra all night.

I toss the shirt to the floor and look at him standing by the door with his fists clenched at his side.

"Naughty, naughty girl. Daddy is going to have to punish you for teasing him all night. Those fucking shorts, the knee-high socks, and now no bra? Oh, sweetheart, that's ten spankings for sure."

I can't help the violent shudder that rips through me, and he stops to check in, "You okay, baby girl?"

"Yes, Daddy. Please." Unsure just what I'm asking for.

"Oh, baby girl, don't you worry." He dips down to lick along my neck to my ear, where he softly whispers, "I'll give you everything. Give me a color first: red, yellow, or green?"

I don't even pause for a breath before blurting, "Green!

Green. So green."

Standing, he slips back into his role as I feel my face heating from my blatant desperation, "Good girl. Did I tell you to stop stripping?"

"No, Daddy. But you should take your clothes off too, get comfy." Teasing, I keep on, "Stay a while."

"If I take my clothes off right now, there's nothing stopping me from throwing you down and rutting into you like an animal. No, I'll strip when I'm good and ready."

I pout, disappointed I can't see him naked yet.

"Don't give me that lip. It'll get bitten. Now, get naked and lie on your back."

I follow his orders, watching his eyes darken. I strip the spanx off and go to strip the socks before he stops me. "Leave them."

Following his lead is easier than I thought it would be, and much more enjoyable than doing it myself. I lay in the middle of the bed and wait.

He comes to the side of the bed and lightly traces the curve of my breast with his fingers, following the lines down to my navel. He stops there, following the rest of the way with his eyes as he pushes my legs wide. I shift my legs, trying to pull them closed when his hand shoots out to stop me.

His voice is a growl, "Don't hide from me, baby girl. Never from me."

He drops his hands to remove his shirt, and my mouth goes dry at the sight before me.

How the fuck does he find time to make himself look like this?

Eight, *yes, I counted*, abs stare back at me. That deliciously lickable V taunting me. I can't hold off; I have to touch him. I lean forward and grab the waist of his jeans. He's stunned still, so I take my chance and run my tongue over that V, trailing down as far as his pants will let me.

These damn things need to go. Now.

"Twelve."

"Worth it."

"You say that now…"

"Promises. Promises," I taunt.

"Fourteen."

Maybe I should stop talking. Ten was manageable, twelve doable, fourteen might be pushing it.

Let's find out.

"Touch me, Daddy. Please. Please touch me."

Apparently, I'm not above begging.

My eyes follow him greedily as he says, "You beg for Daddy so prettily, sweet girl." I swear he's teasing.

He better not be teasing. *If he is, I'm gonna…*

Suddenly, his tongue swipes me from my belly button down to my pussy, "Ungh!"

What the fuck was that sound? *Was that me?*

He repeats the action back up the way he went, and I hear the sound again.

Guess it was me.

"Please, Daddy. Lick me."

And boy, does he!

He starts at my entrance, lazing his way up to my clit where he teases the tight bud. I arch into his teasing lips, seeking more. *More.* I need so much more. And he gives it to me.

He latches on to my clit and takes long, sucking pulls, forcing my hips up off the bed. He's having none of that, though, and wraps his arms around my thighs, pulling me back down. When he has me on the mattress, he stands, taking his mouth off me, and I start to sputter out an indignant response. Before I can even draw a full breath, he's pulled me to the edge of the bed and put my legs over his shoulders.

Looking up at me from between my spread thighs, he says, "That's better," and dives in.

Now I understand why it's called eating out. He's treating this as though he's never tasted anything better. I'm mumbling unintelligible words, pleas that fall on deaf ears. *Probably because of my thighs.*

The things he's doing with his mouth must be divine gifts. I'd say heaven-sent, but this has the Devil written all over it. He spears me with his tongue, thrusting in and out in what I imagine to be an imitation of what he's going to do with his cock. I tense around his tongue at the thought of his cock. In my hands, my mouth, my pussy, all of it. He latches on to my clit again and groans. The sound sends vibrations all through my aching pussy.

I need to come.

I can feel it building and evidently, so can Landon.

He pulls away with a smirk. "Not yet, baby. I didn't give you permission."

"Please? I'm so close. So so close."

"No, you teased Daddy. Remember? You disobeyed and touched me when I told you to lie on the bed. You mouthed off." The grin he gives me seals the deal, his gifts are from the Devil himself, "You earned 14 spankings. Are you ready for your punishment?" He's checking in, making sure I'm still okay with this.

And Lord help me, I am. I am *so* okay with this.

"I'm ready, Daddy."

"Good girl." What is it about that phrase that makes my nipples harden?

Later. I'll think later.

"Come lie across my lap." He sits on the end of the bed, waiting for me to comply. Once I lay across his legs, he grabs my hips to adjust me, so my pelvis is laid against the side of his legs, forcing my ass across his thighs, while my stomach touches the other side.

"You're going to count for me. Do you understand?"

"Yes, Daddy"

"If at any point, you need to stop, say 'red' and everything stops. No questions asked. Understand?"

"I understand, Daddy."

"Good. Start counting."

He starts on my right cheek. *SMACK.*

"One,"

SMACK. Okay, that one left a twinge. Left cheek.

"Two."

SMACK. Fuck! He just spanked my pussy!

I choke out, "Three," and this time, he thrusts two fingers inside me with one hand while the other squeezes the abused flesh.

"Shit, baby. You're so wet." The lewd noise of my own arousal is a little embarrassing. "So wet. So fucking tight. So fucking *mine*."

On and on it went, same pattern, over and over. By the end, I've got silent tears running down my face, and my pussy is on fire with the heat of his hand and dripping with my arousal. Landon lifts me off his lap and arranges me to face him in a straddle. My hot, abused pussy rubs against his pants, and my swollen clit begs for more. I shouldn't be so turned on, but I am.

Oh well. Not thinking about that yet.

"You did so well, baby girl." He says, kissing away a tear. "You took your punishment like the good girl I know you are." Another kiss, another tear.

My tears are no longer silent and I sob out, "Thank you, Daddy." I don't even know why I'm crying so hard. The spanking hurt, yeah, but not so much to warrant this level of crying. Landon lets me cry until I run out of tears and I'm taking stuttering breaths against his chest.

"You needed that, didn't you, sweetheart?"

I didn't even realize, but yeah. I did. I've been carrying around so much, I didn't even realize the kind of release the spanking gave me until he mentioned it. I look back at him, nodding as I say, "Yeah, I think I did. Thank you, Daddy."

"Anything for my baby girl." He kisses my lips languidly, like he has all the time in the world. As I start to settle more, the arousal comes back like a gale force wind.

Strong and all consuming. *I still need to come.*

I start to ride his clothed cock even harder, but right before I reach the peak, he flips us over and disappears back between my legs. He takes a deep breath, and I know he can smell the arousal running down my thighs.

Looking up, he asks, "Color?"

My answer is firm and sure when I say, "Green."

He gets an indulgent smile on his face before he uses that devilish tongue to lick up my thighs, cleaning it of all traces of what was there, before plunging back inside my pussy. The way he eats me is like nothing else. I can't form a single thought. *I don't want to.* I'm just grunting like a fucking cavewoman. I reach down between my legs and spear my fingers through his hair, tugging him where I want him most. He follows without hesitation. While he suctions down on my clit, he shoves two fingers inside my tight, clamping pussy. Stroking along the front wall, searching. And when he finds that magic spot he's looking for, everything goes white. All thought flees from my mind, sound becomes white noise, and my vision goes black as I come harder than I've ever come before.

Then, nothing.

I'm floating.

I faintly feel shifting from between my legs, and then something warm gently wiping, cleaning me. I think I drift off for a minute, because the next thing I know, I'm being wrapped up in corded arms and pulled against a strong, firm frame. As I finally drift off, I hear Landon say something, but I can't quite make out what it is.

I'll ask him in the morning.

CHAPTER 15

Landon

I slowly wake from a deep, satisfying sleep. The way she responded to my touch, the way her skin glowed and warmed under my ministrations had me aching in a way I've never felt before.

She tastes *divine*.

I've never tasted something so indulgent before. She passed out after she came on my tongue—a beautiful display, truly—before we could go any further. Some might be upset about not getting to finish, but those who do, have never had an experience like that.

It was transcendent, life-affirming, soul-searing. She has managed to bind me to her mind, body, and soul. *I love her.* I told her last night, but I think she was already asleep. I'll tell her every day for the rest of our lives, though, so it's okay.

I blindly reach out to the side to pull Hope to my chest, not wanting to open my eyes to the muted lights coming in through the curtains, but my hands find empty sheets instead. They're not cold, so she must've just got up. My sleep-addled brain slowly starts to come back online when I feel the searching hands between my legs, soft fingers caressing up my inner thigh, making the muscles jump and clench.

That has my brain kicking into gear.

I reach down and feel the thickness of Hope's coppery locks, right before her tongue licks my slit.

My hips buck upward, searching for her warm, wet mouth, the action drawing a soft giggle from her tantalizing, full lips. She slowly licks a path from my base to my tip, giving a soft sucking pull before releasing me to run her hand around my shaft.

The brain that had just come online for the day, stutters out again.

My thoughts are shifting too wildly for me to get any words out. I want to tell her she doesn't have to do this, that we can get out of bed and start our day. But I can't make the words come out; the only sounds I seem capable of are grunts.

I really do try to be gentle with her. I'm not a small man by the average standard, and I'm a little thicker than most (or so I've been told), which has posed a problem to some in the past. Once she wraps those lips around me and sucks down *hard,* all thoughts stop. All sounds cease. And my lungs freeze in my chest.

Fuck, she's good at that.

I let out a tortured groan when she pulls off. She slowly fixes her grip, making it tight enough that I start fucking up into her fist without conscious thought.

It feels so fucking good. Then, she lowers her mouth back to my tip. Giving a teasing lick to the slit before her hand stops and her mouth lowers, and lowers, and lowers. I've hit the back of her throat, and *fuck me,* she apparently doesn't have a gag reflex.

She doesn't stop at the back of her throat, though, no. She lowers herself even further, forcing my cock down *into* her throat and holding there. *Then she swallows.* She grabs the hand fisting the sheet next to us and brings it to the exposed column of her neck, placing my fingers on the bulge. All these sensations pull a choked gasp from my lips that *might* be her name, or a prayer to any deity listening that I don't blow my load this quickly.

She reaches one hand under her chin and gently cups my sack, softly lifting their weight and letting it settle back down. On and on she goes, sucking and caressing. Pulling off to jerk me until I'm about to black out from pleasure before releasing me to draw my cock back to her lips.

Through hooded eyes, she looks up at me, "You gave me so much pleasure last night that I passed out and couldn't return the favor." With a devious glint, she continues, "Now I will." She falls back on my cock, down to the base, and starts to suck me enthusiastically.

I can feel the orgasm building in the base of my spine, a tingling spreading upward the closer I get. I try to pull her off, but she just sucks harder and moans. The vibrations cause me to choke out a rough, "Hope," in warning. All she does is hum and redouble her efforts. When I come, it's with a bolt of lightning. My vision turns white, my toes go numb, and I can't catch a full breath for a solid minute. Hope eagerly sucks down everything I give her, as if she's half-starved and this is the first meal she's been given in days.

When the last tremors leave me, I take a shuddering breath to steady myself. Once I've regained the use of my limbs and my vision returns, I turn to pull her up, only to find her propped on her elbow watching me with a sparkle in her eyes. Throwing an arm around her naked waist, I groan, "You're trying to kill me. That's got to be the reason for that...that...I have no words. That was incredible." After all we've done in the last twelve hours, I find it amusing that my praise still makes her blush.

***

We spent the rest of our Saturday trying to keep up with Lizzie. For something so tiny, how is there that much energy? It doesn't make sense! We spent the morning with breakfast, educational TV, and toys. Around 11:00 a.m., we left the house to go to the park to let her play on the playground. *I swear I saw that magazine reporter while we were there, but I can't be sure.* After that, we were home for lunch and a nap by 1:00 p.m.

What I thought would be a blissful, quiet time to recover from the morning's chaos, was *actually* the time Hope uses to get the house picked up, the kitchen cleaned, the groceries ordered, and the floors swept, vacuumed, and mopped. By the time she finished with all of that, Lizzie was waking up after a two-and-a-half hour nap and it was time to start all over again. We had a light snack, put something on Disney+, and relaxed for about thirty minutes while Lizzie shook off the post-nap fog.

At around 4:30 p.m., Hope started making dinner. I didn't understand why she was cooking so early until five o'clock came, and Lizzie started saying and signing that she wanted to eat. It was adorable, until she started screaming and pulling on Hope's clothes when she didn't get her food right away.

I could see the frayed edges of Hope's nerves. She was reaching her limit for the day, and we still had the evening routine to go through. Being mindful of her frayed nerves and the fact that Lizzie wasn't my daughter, "What can I do to help?"

She started to tell me not to worry about it when I cut her off, "I know you can do it yourself, but I'm here telling you that you don't have to. I'm offering an extra set of hands. Let me do this for you."

When that didn't appear to work, I changed tactics. Dropping my voice to a low rumble I leaned close, "Baby girl, I asked you a question. What can I do to help make my baby's evening better?"

Eyes wide and starting to shimmer, she says, "Serve up dinner for us while I get the dishwasher unloaded." She adds a soft "Please," as an afterthought.

Nodding, I kiss her forehead as I reach for the plates in the cabinet and murmur in her ear, "Good girl."

As dinner winds down and the evening routine begins, I can see Hope starting to check out, moving on autopilot. I can only imagine how tired she is, but she's trying her hardest to keep up. I clean the kitchen while she gives Lizzie a bath and gets her ready for bed. I'm just finishing when Hope comes back down the stairs wearing her comfy pants and one of my t-shirts. I rake my gaze over her, appreciating the way my shirt swallows her whole, glaring at the offending pants. She doesn't need the pants; my shirt fits her like one of those minidress things I've seen on women at clubs. She walks into the kitchen, probably thinking she's going to do the dishes, and freezes. She looks from the clean space to me and back again with a comically confused expression. She looks back at me and says, "Thank you, you didn't have to clean the kitchen. I was coming back down to do that myself."

I smile, shaking my head at her.

My voice gentle, "I know I didn't *have* to, baby girl, but I wanted to help. I helped make the mess and I'm perfectly capable of cleaning it up." She's giving me a deer in the headlights look that is easily the cutest thing I've seen today, including when Lizzie cuddled up between us on the couch after her nap.

Walking up to her, I grab her hand and pull her to the couch, where I nearly force her to sit. Pulling her feet into my lap, I sit on the coffee table across from her. "Hope, baby. I love spending time with you and Lizzie. I love getting the little moments like we had this afternoon, but sweetheart, if you continue running yourself ragged this way, you are you might miss out."

She tenses and tries to pull away from me, but I'm not done yet.

"I'm not critiquing your parenting, Hope. I would never begrudge you the way you've adapted to your new reality after Matt died. What I'm trying, and apparently failing, to say is that I love you, Hope; you and Lizzie both. I loved our time together this morning at breakfast, and watching you play with her at the park. If you'd allow me, I'd like to step in and help you. With naptime cleaning, making dinner, and cleaning the kitchen. I'm not the best singer, so I don't know how effective I would be during the song portion of the evening, but I'd be happy to try if you're okay with it. If you're willing to allow someone who loves you to step in and love you the way you deserve. I could see you lagging, the later it got. When you start to feel like that, I want to be able to step in and lift you both up."

She sits there staring at me for so long that I start to get nervous that I've pushed too far. She blinks a few times to clear the shock from her brain and replies,

"Landon, I love you too, I really do. I think Matt would've really liked you, and I can't think of anyone better suited to step in, if that's really something you want to do. But you've only spent the night once. Are you sure that's something you want to sign up for? It's a big responsibility. Maybe you should take time to think about it before you go signing away your life, your freedom."

"I don't have to think about it anymore than I already have. I've known from the moment you opened your door to me that first time, and I got to watch the two of you together. You're both mine. Mine to protect. Mine to love. *Mine.* I wouldn't have it any other way, sweetheart."

She still seems wary, "If you're sure...?"

"I'm sure."

CHAPTER 16

Hope

THREE MONTHS LATER

Things with Landon are amazing. Since that first night, we've spent as much time together as possible. Sometimes he has to work late, and when he does, he'll have dinner sent over for us, so I don't have to cook. Just another way he likes to take care of us. It's been nice, not having to shoulder everything on my own.

Except today. I didn't tell him what today was, and I'm not sure I will.

I've spent all morning in a daze, completing my work on autopilot and not really engaging in conversation with anyone in the office. Diana stopped by to talk to Landon and James about an incoming agent, reviewing paperwork, and the like.

We've gotten really close over the months I've worked here. She started out pretty wary. Either thinking I was with Landon for his money or that this would implode and she would have an HR crisis on her hands. After convincing her that I was only interested in the man himself, we started hanging out. We go to lunch together when Landon is caught up with work. Either in the break room or out at a nearby restaurant. Not today, though.

"Hey, Hope! You wanna go grab some Mexican food after

this meeting?"

I give her what I hope passes as a smile, "Not today. Thanks though!"

Apparently, my smile wasn't convincing enough. "What's wrong? Did something happen with Landon? I swear, that man can be so thickheaded..."

I interrupt her ranting, "No! God, no. Everything with Landon is great, honest. It's just some personal stuff. Don't sweat it!"

She narrows her eyes at me, searching for what I'm hiding. I keep up my almost-smile and remind her, "If you don't get in there on time, you know James will start giving you hell for being late."

At that, she rolls her eyes. "He could use a lesson in patience. It won't kill him to wait five minutes while I check in with my friend." Casting her gaze towards me, she shifts the conversation back to me and plops down on my desk, "And don't try to change the subject! Now, tell me what's wrong."

"What's wrong with who?"

Shit. I forgot Landon had gotten up to run downstairs for a coffee.

Without breaking eye contact, Diana rats me out. "Something is wrong with your girl here, and she won't tell me what it is."

Landon's head jerks to me, and with a scowl, he damn near growls, "What happened?"

Closing my eyes and praying for the strength to be convincing enough to get him into his meeting, I return my eyes to his, "Nothing happened," *recently,* "I promise, I'm alright. Y'all go get to your meeting."

Landon's eyes search my face for the truth, and because the man can read me like the pages of a book, he tells me, "Come with me. We're going home."

Wait. What?

"What? No, we're not! It's the middle of the day, and you have meetings for the rest of the afternoon."

As I speak, Landon is gathering my things from my desk and, without pausing to glance at her, asks, "Diana, I know it's not your job, but could you please reschedule my meetings? You and James can discuss the new hire without me. I believe James' afternoon is fairly open. If there are any meetings that can't be moved, give them to him. Tell him I'm taking Hope home."

She doesn't miss a beat, "You got it!"

"Diana!" I exclaim, completely put off that this is all happening as if I'm not standing right here.

She ignores me, "I'll take care of everything, you take care of her."

"I'm standing right here, you know!"

They both continue to ignore my outbursts, "I plan to."

With that seemingly settled, Landon hauls my things over one shoulder and turns to me, "Sweetheart, we're going home. You can either walk out of here on your own, or I can throw you over my shoulder and walk you out myself."

My eyes bug out, because I know he's serious, so I huff and, through gritted teeth, tell him, "I'll walk." Turning, I storm out, not waiting to see if he's following.

In the car with no way to escape the inquisition I know is coming, I do the only thing my normally rational brain can think of. I give him the silent treatment. Of course, that only works when the person on the receiving end is trying to talk to you. We pull up to my house in what seems like no time at all. We get out of the car and walk up the drive.

Landon digs the keys out of my purse and unlocks the door to let us in. The house is silent since Lizzie is at school and my mom is picking her up for me. "Go upstairs. I want you to take a shower and lie face down on the bed when you're done."

Not today, Satan. I am *so* not in the mood to play.

"Landon, I really don't want—"

He cuts me off, "Nope. Don't argue with me, Hope. You lied to me. You said there wasn't anything wrong, and there very clearly is. *Go.*"

"I'm not fucking you like this!"

"Hope, I'm losing my patience. Did I say anything about fucking?"

I stay silent, thinking the question was rhetorical. It wasn't.

"Well? Did I?"

"No."

"No, what?"

I sigh, "No, Daddy. You didn't say anything about fucking me."

"And what did Daddy say?"

"You told me to go take a shower and lie face down on the bed."

"Good, so you did listen to me. Why haven't you done it yet?"

Rolling my eyes, I turn my back and march to the shower.

"Oh, fuck that."

I don't see him coming. Next thing I know, I'm being pushed against the nearest wall, and my pants are being yanked down. Once they're around my knees, he gives me three hard and fast swats, leaving my flesh tingling.

"What the fuck, Landon?!" I screech. I could safeword and he would back off, I know he would. I'm not entirely sure why I don't, given my current state, I probably shouldn't entertain this but here we are.

Why am I like this?

His voice is low, and gruff when he replies, "You did not just roll your eyes at me. I *know* you didn't." His voice drops impossibly lower, and he roughly squeezes my stinging ass, "But since I'm not one to disregard what I saw with my own eyes, you're going to be punished for that little display." His next words growled in my ear, "Go to your room. *Now.*"

CHAPTER 17
Landon

I can't believe she did that! She really rolled her eyes at me, and after lying to me on top of that?

Fuck that.

She's getting the punishment of a lifetime, and my cock couldn't be more thrilled at the thought. I wait in the living room for her to finish her shower, trying and failing to figure out what she's hiding. She's slowly withdrawn all week, and I honestly can't say I would've noticed if I didn't practically live with her.

My house is nice and all, but it's not a *home*. It doesn't have the lived-in feel to it that Hope's does. Nothing particularly personal is on display in my house, no deeply-sentimental touches. My family was great growing up, I really can't complain, but I'm the only one left. My mom couldn't get pregnant after me because of the ovarian cysts, and she decided to have a full hysterectomy to get ahead of the cancer risks, so she didn't even have the option to have another kid afterward. Dad worked hard, but was always home for dinner, always there to help tuck me in at night, and there to bail me out of trouble with the other kids' parents as I got older. They both passed at the blessedly old age of 85, my dad two years before my mom. I have photo albums, but only a couple of framed pictures of us as a family in my room and home office.

Hope's pulling away all week has been driving me nuts,

but any time I've asked she's insisted she was fine.

Fine. Worst and most troubling word in the English language; so small yet so loaded. I stop my pacing when I hear my phone ring.

"Hey James, is everything okay at the office?"

"Dude, forget about the office. Diana and I have got it covered. Is Hope okay? Di said she was upset but wouldn't talk to her, and then you just up and left to take her home. We're worried about her."

God, I love my friends.

"I think she's alright. I know she's not sick, so physically she's fine. But something is going on, I just don't know what yet. She's been retreating into herself all week..." I trail off, "You know what? Let me call you tomorrow. I think I know who can help."

"Yeah, man. Let me know if there's anything we can do to help."

I'm not even really hearing him anymore, my mind is already on my next steps.

After hanging up with James, I looked through Hope's bag for her phone. *God, I hope they don't get mad at me.* She doesn't keep a password on it, so it's easy to open and access the FaceTime app. I dial Katy and Ginny, hoping they can help me figure this out.

Ginny answers first, "Hey lovey, oh!"

Katy comes on next, "Hey, uh, Landon?"

"Hey, ladies, sorry to bother you. I was hoping you could help me out with something."

They hesitate for a second, "Hope is in the shower. I made her go up there to relax for a minute. Something is going on with her. She won't tell me, and I can't figure it out. Do either of you know? Has she said anything?"

Katy answers, "No, she hasn't mentioned anything to me...Wait." Her eyes go wide, "Ginny, what's today's date?!"

Ginny closes her eyes on an exhale and whispers, "Crap. I didn't realize what today was." She shakes her head with a defeated look on her face. For a minute, no one says anything.

"Ladies, please. I'm lost here."

They exchange a glance between them before Katy says, "Tell him, Gin. She won't. She'll try to do this on her own again. And we both know how that ended last time."

"Should I be worried?"

Ginny sighs, "For her physical being? Not really. She won't do anything extreme, but she might try to drink herself stupid, as a way to cope."

"Cope with *what*, Ginny? What is going on?" I'm starting to lose my patience with the cryptic shit.

She narrows her eyes on me, "Watch your tone, Landon. I like you, you're good for her. But I won't let you get pissy with me."

"Sorry. Truly, I am. Please, just tell me what's going on."

"Landon, it's the second anniversary of Matt's death."

Oh.

She goes on, "He died right as Lizzie was turning one. Last year..." she trails off, lost in thought. "Last year was rough. She called us in tears at the beginning of the week and spiraled from there. When Katy and I showed up, Lizzie was with her grandparents, and Hope was on the couch, eyeballs deep in wine. It wasn't a pretty sight. She said she had accepted his death, that that wasn't her biggest issue. Yeah, she was still upset—who wouldn't be?—but what upset her the most was the milestones Matt would miss with Lizzie. Lizzie's birthday is on Friday; if she's just now showing outward signs of how upset she is, she's already better off than last year. Like I said, you're good for her. I don't know what triggered it this time, but you just need to be there for her."

I nod, reeling from the information too much to verbalize a response.

I need to tread lightly. I thank the girls and hang up, making one more phone call.

On the second ring, there's an answer, "Hey, honey, how're you doing? I didn't expect to hear from you today."

"Sorry to bother you, Mrs. Long. It's Landon."

"Oh, hello, Landon. Is Hope okay? Is she hurt?" She sounds a little panicked. Maybe I should've led with *"everything is okay."*

"No ma'am, she's physically fine. I was calling to ask you a favor."

"What is it?"

"Would Lizzie be able to sleep over tonight? I just found out from Ginny and Katy what today is, and Hope isn't dealing with it very well. I wanted to give her some time to mourn, if that's what she needs."

There's a pause on the line, "What day is...oh. Of course she can. She has a ton of stuff over here already, so don't worry about her. We won't even stop by for a bag."

"Thank you, ma'am."

"Of course, but please, call me Maria."

"Maria. Thank you so much. I'll make it up to you and Jace."

"You don't have to thank me. Take care of her."

"I will." *Forever if she'll let me*, but I don't say that out loud.

With that mystery solved, it's time to punish my baby girl for lying to me. I turn and head up the stairs. Even knowing that she's hurting, I'm excited for what I have planned. She needs a release, and I plan on giving her many tonight.

Coming to the closed door, I knock as I open it. Walking in, I see her on the bed, covered in a blanket.

Damn, I took too long on the phone.

"Sorry it took me so long, baby girl. Thank you for listening to me and waiting."

She doesn't answer. *Fine, we can play it that way.* Walking to her nightstand, I pull out one of her vibrators, the kind that vibrates on her g-spot while air pulses on her clit.

"Here's what's going to happen. Daddy is going to spank you fifteen times or until your ass is glowing — whichever happens first, then I'm going to stuff you with this vibrator and turn it on. You'll lay here with the vibrator running, but you're not allowed to come, not until I say. Do you understand? If you come, you'll stand in the corner for twenty minutes with your nose to the wall and your ass out."

Her breathing has deepened and turned ragged, "Yes, Daddy." Her eyes are as dark as night, and she licks her lips in anticipation.

That's my girl.

I slowly approach the bed, shedding my jacket, shoes, and socks. My shirt is the next to go. I undo my cuffs and the buttons down the front before sliding it off my shoulders. I'm tempted to use my belt on her ass, to see the stripes of red against the creamy white, but I want to feel the heat of each strike too much to deny myself. Besides, Hope needs the connection, even if she doesn't realize it yet.

The first strike I deliver is merely a warmup, enough to make her jump, but not enough to sting. I strike again and again, alternating sides, working top to bottom.

Right side, bottom. Repeat on the left.

Right side, middle. Repeat on the left.

Right side, top. Repeat on the left.

At the end of the pattern, I roughly squeeze the reddened flesh, enjoying the harsh inhale she gives. I spank her until the skin of her ass glows in the dim lighting, like the sun trying to peek through the curtains, she takes all fifteen beautifully. After the tenth spank, I can feel her silent cries. After fifteen, she doesn't bother stifling her sobs. I pause in my lashings, letting her breathe.

"Please, Daddy. Please."

I can't help but give myself a slight grin. She's ready.

"You did so well, baby girl. Daddy is so proud of you." I pull her up so we're chest to chest, skin to skin, letting her rest her head on my shoulder. "We're almost done, sweetheart."

She sniffles, trying to gather herself. I don't want her to shut down again, so I quickly stand, holding firmly to the abused flesh of her ass. She hisses and tries to launch away from me, but has nowhere to go. I lay her down on the bed, and Hope sucks in air through clenched teeth when her backside rubs against the soft comforter.

I run my hands over her hips, across her pelvis, and down between her legs. Her pussy is weeping for me. Running my fingers through her folds, I gather her wetness and bring it to my lips. Moaning at the taste of her.

Not yet.

Pushing my desires down, I grab the vibrator and turn it on. I run the tip through her lips, teasing her hard little clit before bringing it to her entrance and pushing in.

She gasps at the intrusion, and I flip on the little rabbit vibe attached to the main piece, letting it lightly rest against her clit. I leave her there for a moment, relishing in her gasps and moans as she gets closer and closer to the edge. Before she can fall over, I pull the vibrator out.

"No, no, no, little girl. You don't get to come. Do you know why?"

She's nothing but a wanton, blubbering mess, and I've never loved her more.

"Daddy asked a question. Do you know why you're being punished?"

"Yes, Daddy. I'm sorry, Daddy. I'm sorry I rolled my eyes. Please, please let me come. I'm so close. So close." She's nearly sobbing again from the pleasure taken away from her.

"Try again. Why aren't you allowed to come?"

She shakes her head, tears creating new tracks down her face. She knows now that I know what's going on, but she won't admit it out loud.

"Fine, let's go again. Remember, you don't get to come.

Not until you can tell me why you're being punished." With that, I push the vibrator back inside her pussy, so swollen and dripping with her arousal. I watch her writhe on the bed, see her begin to roll her hips to ride the toy. Just when she throws her head back, I pull it out again.

"Please, Daddy, please. I'm sorry. I'm sorry. I'm sorry."

She keeps repeating that she's sorry while her pussy pulses, looking for something to grip.

"Why are you being punished, baby girl?"

She doesn't answer, just keeps apologizing and begging to come.

"Again." Once more, I push the vibrator inside her. I don't even have a second to take my hand away from the toy before she comes. It's a beautifully violent explosion. Her head is thrown back, back arched, and thighs tense. Her face, neck, and chest are red from the scream she releases. I stand there, both disappointed that she came and giddy at the fact that she couldn't hold it back.

Sighing, "Go stand in the corner. Nose to the wall. And be sure you stick that ass out. I want to admire my work."

She gets up on shaky limbs to do as she's told and as she passes me, I murmur, "Good girl."

When she gets to the corner of the room and arranges herself, I sit on the bed doing just what I told her I would and admire my marks on her skin. Some are starting to fade, but that's fine, I can always add more. I run my hand over my dick through my pants, trying to adjust, and nearly come from the sensation.

I stand to walk over to her. Vibrator in hand, I stand behind her. "You're going to stand here until you answer me.

And every time you don't, I'm going to edge you again, closer and closer without letting you come. Are we clear?"

I give her ass a little swat when she doesn't answer right away. She jumps and replies with a mumbled, "Yes, Daddy."

"Good. So, will you tell me what's been bothering you all week, or are we going to stand here all night?"

Sniffling, she tries again to deny it. "Nothing is going on! I'm fine!"

Tsk. Tsk. Tsk. "Five minutes."

I widen her stance with a nudge of my foot to her ankles. Pushing on her upper back, I lower her until her ass is pushing against me. "Keep your nose to the wall, princess."

With her open to me, I glide the head of the vibrator back inside and turn it on. She tries to pull away from it, to avoid the pleasure that's being pushed on her so soon after her last orgasm, but can't with me holding on to the back of her neck.

"Nuh-uh, pretty girl. Five minutes, and you don't get to come." I pause, "Unless, of course, you want to talk to me."

The time passes quickly, for me anyway. As I watch the minutes tick, I notice her switch from trying to jerk away from the vibrations to trying to push back into them. Her attempts are cute, but I'm holding the vibrator out of reach each time she tries to sway, by the end Hope is panting and starting to sweat. Her arousal is steadily running down her leg, so I ask again. "What's going on in that pretty head of yours, Hope?"

She stubbornly shakes her head again, but her resolve is breaking. I can see it in the clenched fist against the wall, in the shaking of her knees.

Almost there.

"Fine, another round then. Shall we say ten minutes?"

She releases a tired, heaving breath, and we go again.

After that time is up, I can see the strain in the way her muscles are clenched. She's trying so hard not to come, just to avoid telling me what we both know I already know. When I ask again, she once more shakes her head.

"Fifteen minutes. I can do this all night, baby girl." I lean down in her space, covering her sensitized body with my own. "I will keep going, you need to come, baby. I can see it, feel it, smell it. All you have to do is tell me."

This time, she breaks. After three minutes, she nearly drops to the floor screaming. The only thing holding her in place is me pressed against her backside and my hand on the back of her neck. She comes so hard, she squirts all over the floor. And still, she comes more. Slowly, she starts coming down from her orgasm, aftershocks racking her body.

I gently lift her, placing her on the bed and walk away to grab a warm cloth to clean her up. When I get back to the bed, she's lying on her side holding her knees.

"On your back, baby. Let me get you cleaned up." She numbly complies, and when she starts to speak, it's nothing more than a broken whisper.

CHAPTER 18

Hope

I don't remember getting in the bed. I don't remember Landon stripping naked and bringing me into his chest. I just remember the pain of his hand mixed with blinding pleasure. I hear a hollow voice begin to speak.

"You know, don't you?"

"Yeah, baby girl. I knew something was up, and you wouldn't tell me, so I made a few phone calls."

I turn over to face him, burrowing into his neck as I sigh in resignation of what I have to tell him.

"They only know he died in a car accident. Everyone was so focused on me and Lizzie; they didn't ask for many details." Hiccupping, I continue, "I told everyone it was instant. Even asked the doctors to spare his parents the details so they wouldn't have to live with the images I do."

He sucks in a breath, holding it in anticipation of what I'm about to say.

"I got the call from the hospital, called my parents to watch Lizzie, telling them there was an accident and I needed to go. When I got to the hospital and saw Matt lying there in the bed, I knew he wouldn't make it through the surgery they were prepping him for. I honestly didn't think he would make it to the operating theater. He didn't either."

I pause to let out a ragged sob, "He told me he was sorry, but he wouldn't be able to make it home in time to kiss me goodnight. That he wouldn't be able to make us breakfast in the morning like he always did when he worked late and missed dinner."

I wipe the tears from my face, looking him in the eye for this next part. "I held his hand as he died. I watched the life fall from his face. The nurses came in to try to save him, but they couldn't. Too much internal damage, or something like that. I went and sat in the hall in front of his room and sobbed. I don't know how long I sat there, but eventually one of the EMTs that brought him in came and sat beside me. He didn't say anything, just sat there with me."

I got up from the bed and went to the jewelry box next to the dresser, opening it as I continued to relive that night. "The EMT handed me two crumpled pieces of paper. Nothing very big. I recognized the handwriting and lost it again. Matt had written two letters in the trauma bay. Apparently, the adrenaline hadn't worn off yet. He had the EMT give them to me when I got there. One was for me, telling me he loved Lizzie and me and that he was sorry he wouldn't be around for any more milestones or anniversaries."

I stop to take a breath as I climb back into bed, sitting against the headboard next to Landon. "The other was for you."

I hand him the letter as he sits up next to me.

"For me?" He asks, confusion written all over his face.

"It was for the man who would come after him. The one he would want to take care of his daughter in his stead. The one he hoped I would find that would make today a little easier, more manageable." Looking up at his shimmering eyes through my tear-soaked lashes, I silently plead for him to be that man. To take me, emotional scars and all, and to take my daughter. To love her as Matt did, and as only a man of his caliber could.

He reaches out a shaky hand to open the letter, but I stick my own out to stop him.

"Please, not right now. Not with me here, at least. That's between you and Matt, I don't need to know what's in it, nor do I want to."

He nods, a bit mechanically, while setting the letter on the nightstand and pulling me close. He kisses the top of my head as he lowers us to lie back down. As I start to drift, I remember that I need to get Lizzie from school and bolt upright to start dressing. "Settle back down, sweetheart. I called your mom. She's got our little munchkin tonight. We can go get her tomorrow."

I lean my head back to kiss his jaw. "I love you."

"I love you too, Hope. And Lizzie. More than you'll ever know."

At that declaration, my releases take their toll, and I drift off. Finally feeling a semblance of peace for the first time since Matt died, like a weight has been lifted off my chest...maybe I don't have to do this alone after all.

CHAPTER 19

Landon

I was prepared for a lot, going into that conversation. I was not, however, prepared for *that*.

She hides it well, the exhaustion, the heartache. I don't know that I would've been that strong in her position. It makes me love her more. The way she wholeheartedly loves, without reservation, or fear, I want to be deserving of that kind of devotion.

She's been asleep for an hour or so now. Careful not to wake her, I untangle our limbs and slip out of bed. Grabbing a pair of sweats from the drawer she cleaned out for me, I head into the living room with Matt's note in hand.

I'm not sure if I'm ready to read this. But he wrote it for the man he hoped Hope would choose to follow him, so I have to know. Sitting on the couch, I open the envelope:

You're only reading this because I can't be there anymore. And if you are, she's deemed you worthy of her time and energy. Please don't waste it. It also means that you've managed to worm your way into my daughter's heart, too. Congratulations, if she's anything like her mother, it was a feat. One that probably involved bribery of some kind. Part of me hopes she made you work for it, but if she didn't, then you must be someone special.

Hope is a remarkable woman. She will love you with every fiber of her being. She will give you everything and ask for nothing in return.

Give her the world. Give her everything I can't.

Take care of my girls. They are and will always be my whole world and not even death will change that.

Hope will be a guiding light for you. She was for me. And Lizzie, my sweet, sweet Lizzie. Do me a favor? I know I can't hold you to it, but if you're the man she thinks you are, I know you will. Don't let my Lizzie go a single day without knowing how much I loved her. Please.

Treat my girls with the love and respect they deserve.

Best of luck, my friend. You just might need it.

- Matt

Sitting on the couch, I scrub a hand over my face to wipe away the evidence of tears and make a promise to Matt and myself.

I will never let a day go by that I don't tell them how much I love them.

***

It's Lizzie's birthday!

After reading Matt's letter, I find it a little bittersweet. I know Hope is having a hard time with it, so I decided to take them both to see him. I loaded down the car with a mylar balloon, a cupcake, a candle, and a bouquet of fresh-cut flowers. When all of that is stowed away, I go back into the house to get my girls.

Hope is sitting at the table, having a birthday breakfast feast with Lizzie. I sit across from them and take in the perfection unfolding around me. Lizzie is absolutely demolishing her waffles and fruit, taking extra care to get syrup all over everything as she does. Hope, my sweet Hope, is sitting at the table with her mug of coffee to her smiling lips as she watches.

You can see the emotions playing across her face: sadness that Matt isn't here, joy for another birthday with Lizzie, and even a touch of guilt. It plays like a movie that I can't help but watch, and I want to offer her some solace. Anything I can do to make today just a touch easier for her bear.

"Hey Hope?"

She turns to face me, and the tone of my voice must give something away because she tenses, throwing her guard up.

"Yes?"

"I had an idea I wanted to run by you. Something we could do before Lizzie's party…as a family…if you'd like."

Her face softens a fraction at my calling us a family, but her guard is still sky-high.

"What did you have in mind?"

Here goes nothing.

"I wanted to take you and Lizzie to see Matt."

She visibly flinches back in her chair, immediately shaking her head.

"Before you turn it down, will you hear my reasoning?"

She doesn't answer me, but she doesn't tell me no either so I decide to go on, treading *very* lightly.

"If you decide the answer is no, then that's it. But I want you to consider going to celebrate Lizzie with Matt. I've got a cupcake, candle, balloon, and flowers already loaded in the car. I think this would be good for you, and we could make it a tradition with Lizzie. This way, she never forgets her dad. You can tell her stories about the two of you while you were dating, and as she gets older, she can go talk to him when she wants to feel close."

She doesn't say anything for a long time, only sits there watching me, with a look on her face I can't begin to describe.

"I can drop you off and leave while you guys visit, wait in the car, or come with you. Whatever you're comfortable with... What do you think?"

She still doesn't speak.

"If you don't want to, please just tell me and I'll drop it. I only want to help, be there for you —" she raises her hand to cut me off.

She stands and rounds the table, coming to a stop next to me, where she drops down in my lap and gives me an emotion-fueled kiss. I tentatively return it, not totally sure where this is going.

"Thank you," she says. "Thank you for everything. You've become such a major piece of our lives." She turns to Lizzie as she continues, "I think you're right. I think it would be good, for us both, to go celebrate with Matt. Just this first time, do you mind waiting in the car?" She looks down at her hands as if embarrassed. "There are some things I want to say to him..."

She trails off as I lift her chin to look into her silver-blue eyes. "Baby girl, there is nothing in this world I wouldn't do for you or give you," I pause to look at Lizzie and back to Hope, "Either of you. I'll wait as long as you need."

Kissing her nose, I move to stand. "Take your time getting ready. I already told everyone we might be late, and they were all okay with it. In-laws included. They'll all be waiting for us at your parents' house when we're ready." Moving to Lizzie, "I'll take the munchkin, clean her up, and get her dressed." I pause halfway to the stairs and turn back to see a stunned Hope standing in the middle of the dining room, mouth agape. "I love you, Hope Lawson."

CHAPTER 20

Hope

We ride in silence to the cemetery. There's nothing to be said. We have some Disney music playing over the radio for Lizzie, but it's as if even she knows what's going on because she's not even bumping her foot to the music like she usually does. I'm not sure, but I think this stems from Matt's letter to Landon.

He's been a little different since that night. More affectionate, the first one to say I love you in the morning before work, when we drop Lizzie off, before bed, and even just randomly throughout the day. Even with Lizzie. In the four months we've been together, he and Lizzie have become as thick as thieves. Sometimes I catch them in the hall looking at pictures and pointing out the people in them. When they get to a picture of Matt, Landon takes extra time to tell her about her daddy. Even though he doesn't know much about him. He tells her things like, "Your daddy loved you very much, Lizzie Bear;" and "he was a great man. He loved your mommy with all his heart, and he was very sad when he had to go."

In moments like that, I hide around the corner and have to blink back tears. It's just such a tender moment, and he's become so ingrained in our everyday life. I feel a little guilty, being this happy when Matt has only been gone for a little over two years, but I know this is what he would want for me. Looking at Landon as he drives, I know he is who Matt would want for Lizzie and me.

We pull up to the cemetery and park. Landon gets out to help unload Lizzie and everything he bought for this, and when he starts to walk with us, I get nervous about asking him to stay in the car again. I don't want to be rude, since he did all this for us, but he starts before I can say anything.

"I know what you're thinking. I only want to walk you guys over and help set up, so I know where you are. Once you guys are settled, I'll come back to the car and wait."

I let out the breath I was holding. "Thank you, Landon. For everything. For my job, for taking on Lizzie as your own, for taking *me* on, and for this. Just...thank you."

He pulls us to a stop, looks at me, and says, "I don't know how many times I have to tell you, woman. There is literally nothing in this world I wouldn't do for the two of you. In four months, you both have become my center axis. My world spins around the two of you," pausing to pick up Lizzie, "I love you both more than words can say. I hope one day you can accept that, because I've already told you; I'm not letting you go without a fight."

Knowing he doesn't like it, but not having any words, I simply smile and nod, trying my best to hold in the tears threatening to roll down my cheeks.

He narrows his eyes on me and gives me a playful swat, "I'm going to let that slide right now, but only because of little eyes and where we are. After we leave, it's all fair game. Got it?"

Shivering at his tone, I give him what he wants when I lean in to whisper, "Okay, Daddy."

He leans in to kiss me before he kisses Lizzie's cheek, making her giggle, and we start heading to Matt's grave again. He pauses his steps for a brief moment but shakes his head and continues on. I give him a questioning look, wanting to know what that was about, but he just shakes his head again with a slight smile on his face. *Odd.* Once we get there, Landon does exactly what he said. He helps us set everything up, and with one last parting kiss for both of us, walks back to the car.

Landon

I could've sworn I just saw a camera flash out of the corner of my eye, but as I turn to head back to the car, I don't see anything out of the ordinary. I look around for any sign of the woman I think has been following me, but I don't see any women hanging around. *I'm being paranoid.* There's a guy across the cemetery kneeling next to a headstone with his bag off to the side, but that's it.

I'm definitely being paranoid.

I shake my head again to try and clear it out, to wait by the car for my girls to come back to me. Taking a second, I look up at the sky.

"I've got them, Matt. You can rest easy now."

Hope

Sitting here with Lizzie feels both strange and comforting all at the same time. Placing the flowers against the headstone, I sit with Lizzie in my lap and light the candle on the cupcake. I sing Happy Birthday to her, she blows out the candle, and we dig in, eating in silence for a beat.

Eventually, Lizzie turns to me and asks, "Daddy?"

Letting the tears fall freely, I nod, "Yeah, baby, daddy is here with us right now. He wanted to spend your birthday together as a family."

She looks at my tears, a little confused. Patting my cheek, she asks, "You okay?"

Never one to lie to her, "No, baby. Mommy's heart hurts. She misses your daddy a lot but is so happy with Mr. Landon and she feels guilty for being happy. It's all really confusing."

Obviously, she doesn't understand what I just said, but she looks toward the car and points, "Daddy here?"

I'm a little stunned. *Does she think Landon is her dad?*

Shaking my head, I tell her the truth, "No, baby. Your daddy is here." I point to the headstone to show her before I continue, "But I think Mr. Landon wants to try to be a second daddy for you. Think you're okay with that?"

She just points to the car again and shouts, "Daddy!"

I give a watery smile, shake my head, and hug her close before I pull out my phone. It's been about twenty minutes, and I think Lizzie might need a change in scenery given how restless she's becoming. Dialing Landon, I wait for him to pick up.

"Hey princess, everything okay?"

"Hey, yeah. I was wondering if you'd come grab Lizzie? I think she needs a change of scenery, and she misses you."

He's silent for a beat before he continues, "Of course, I'll be over in just a minute."

"Okay, thank you. I won't be much longer."

"What did I say this morning? Take your time. We'll be here when you're ready."

Landon comes to grab Lizzie, and before he walks away, I want to let him know about what Lizzie said. Grabbing his arm, I stop him and blurt out, "Lizzie called you daddy."

Landon's whole body locks down, and I'm terrified that he's about to bolt.

"Okay, um, do I need to correct her?"

Unable to answer that just yet, I turn it back to him.

"Do you want to?" *God, I hope not.* I really want him to stay in our lives. And as much as I love him, it's really conflicting to be having this conversation right here in front of my dead husband's gravestone.

Hesitating, he says, "Honestly, no, I don't. I'm trying really hard not to let the smile that wants to break free split my face in half and start dancing for joy, because I don't know how you feel about it. I love this little girl and will continue to love her for the rest of my life. I would be honored to be her daddy, but if you're not ready for that, we can work on correcting her. She may not even know what she's saying."

I nod and let him know, "I think I might be okay with it. I definitely want you in our lives, and there was something I wanted to talk to you about later on, but I think I want to ease into it. Make sure *you're* ready for everything this entails."

"Baby girl, I told you. You're both mine. I'm ready whenever you are. We go at your pace here." Smiling, he kisses me and starts walking toward the car with Lizzie on his back, "We'll be in the car when you're ready." And with that, he's gone.

Turning back to Matt's grave, I sit and cross my legs.

"Hey Matt. It's Lizzie's birthday today." Sniffling, I keep talking, "She's officially turning three today, can you believe it?" Huffing out a watery laugh, "God, I can't believe you're really gone. I feel so...so..." my sigh is ragged, "I don't know what I feel anymore. I'm sad you're gone, but happy because it's Lizzie's birthday. Then I feel guilty for being happy when you can't be here. To top it all off, I met someone. His name is Landon. He's the one who came to grab Lizzie so we could talk. I think you'd like him. Which is so weird to say out loud...I really like him. Honestly, I love him. I didn't think that was possible after you. I thought you took that piece of my heart with you. And maybe you did, but I think he found another piece for himself. I really hope you were nice in your letter; I know how sarcastic you can be."

I give a lighthearted chuckle at the memories flashing through my mind.

"I feel like maybe you sent him to me, like you picked him yourself, and that's why he's everything I've needed." A gentle breeze blows across my face, and I smile, looking up at the sky. Getting up, I tell him, "Thank you, Matt. For loving me like you did, giving me Lizzie, and sending Landon to me. I love you."

I kiss my fingers and press them to the headstone as I get up to leave. When I turn, I catch a glimpse of something reflecting the sunlight. I don't remember anything reflective being there when we walked in, but maybe someone is here setting up an arrangement or something, so I continue back to the car without a second thought.

As I walk, I feel lighter than I have in a while. Like coming here was exactly what I needed. I slow my steps when I hear someone sniffling to my right. I turn my head to see a woman crumpled on the ground and gasping as she sobs. Slightly concerned, I walk over to her to offer her the napkin in my pocket. Her hair is disheveled, and her clothes are a bit wrinkled, like this is the second day wearing them. She's facing away from me, so I can't see anything else about her, but I tap her on the shoulder anyway.

"Hey, I'm not going to ask if you're okay given where we are, but I have a napkin if you'd like it."

She doesn't turn or speak, just nods her head. I pass the napkin over her shoulder, and she reaches up to accept it, wiping her eyes and blowing her nose. I rest my hand on her shoulder in an attempt at some non-invasive comfort before I move to leave. As I go, I hear a broken, "Thank you."

"You're welcome. I'm sorry for the pain you're feeling. I hope it gets easier."

With that, I head back to the car.

CHAPTER 21

Landon

After Hope came back to the car, there was a lightness to her I hadn't seen before. I guess coming out here helped better than I thought. The ride back is comfortably silent as I let the girls digest what happened, and I digest that Lizzie has taken to calling me daddy. I am absolutely over-the-moon excited, but I am a little nervous about meeting Hope's in-laws now.

Meeting her parents went well when I picked Hope up for our date. Maria was so nice and welcoming, and after getting her father to open up a bit with questions about the woodworking equipment in his garage everything went off without a hitch. I think they really like me, since her dad invited me back to work with him in the garage and Maria told me to come over whenever I wanted, even without the girls.

With her in-laws though, I don't want to upset them if Lizzie calls me daddy in front of them. Their son was her dad, *is* her dad. I don't want them to think I'm replacing him. Needless to say, I'm nervous when we finally pull up to Maria and Jace's house. Ginny and Katy are walking up the front steps when we get there and go straight into the house without knocking. Turning to Hope, I finally admit my nerves, "I don't want to upset your in-laws if Lizzie calls me daddy in front of them. I don't want them to think I'm trying to replace their son. Maybe I should just drop you guys off and come back later, after they leave..."

My ramblings are cut off when Hope kisses me, long and deep. I take a calming breath and apologize.

"I'm sorry, I just don't want to upset anyone."

She cups my cheek and makes sure I'm looking at her when she says, "Breathe with me."

So, I do. I take a few more calming breaths, and then Hope speaks.

"I know you don't want to upset anyone, and I wish I knew what their reaction will be. They're good people, though, so I would like to think they'd be understanding. Especially given that Matt died when Lizzie was so young. She doesn't have any memories of him. We'll get through whatever happens together, though."

I nod, and she gasps mockingly, "Use your words, Landon."

I narrow my eyes and quickly give her thigh a squeeze to tickle her. She shrieks a giggle, trying to worm away from me. She can't get anywhere in the car, so I give her a few more until there's a knock on the window. I look up and see Matt, or rather, an older version of him. I remove my hand quickly, like I've been shocked, and get out to round the side of the car.

Opening Hope's door, I step aside so the two can hug.

"Hey Dan, it's good to see you. Is Cynthia already inside?"

"Hey girl! Yeah, she is. I just pulled up and saw you sitting here." He eyes me warily before a smile splits his face, "Wanted to say hi to my grandbaby before she gets monopolized."

Hope goes to the back to get Lizzie out. When she does, my little girl burrows into her mom's neck to hide behind her hair before she sees me and reaches out. I try to stand back and let her grandfather take her, but she's having none of it.

"Well, don't make the birthday girl mad. Go on and grab her, she'll warm up to me in a bit."

"I'm sorry, sir. We've had an emotional morning..." I cut off, not even thinking about what I was saying before I said it. Panicking, I look to Hope for help.

"Dan, this is Landon. I've been seeing him for a few months, and after I told him about Matt he wanted to take me and Lizzie to see him for her birthday. We're just getting here from the cemetery."

Dan holds out his hand to shake mine. His voice is strained as he utters, "Thank you," and turns to go into the house.

I look to Hope for a clue as to what that means going forward, but all she does is shrug and nod her head toward the house. I reach out to take her hand and notice something out of the corner of my eye that makes my back go straight and my eye twitch. Seeing the change and where I'm glaring, Hope turns to see what's happening.

"Landon? What is it? Is something wrong?"

"I don't know, baby girl, but I'm about to find out. Take Lizzie inside. Now."

"Landon, what is it? I'm getting a little freaked out."

"I'm sorry, baby. I'm not trying to scare you." I let out a sigh and explain, "I think there's a photographer up the street taking pictures of us. I'm going to try to get him to talk to me. Find out who he's shooting for. Take Lizzie inside and keep her face covered. I don't want any pictures of her in the public eye if I can help it."

Hope's face flushes red with fury, and she pulls Lizzie in closer. She grips my hand tighter and says, "Wait here. You're not going over there without one or two other people as witnesses."

My heart stops beating for a second before restarting in a full gallop. In an angry, hushed voice, I whisper-shout, "Hope Lawson, if you think for one second I'm going to let you come over there with me, I swear to all that is holy and sacred in this world I will *blister* your ass!"

She gives me an utterly devious look before she lets out a little giggle, "Oh, Daddy. It won't be me. My dad's best friend, Frank, is here." She huffs out a small laugh, "He'll be just what you need. Wait here."

She dashes off inside the house before I can protest. She's only gone for a few minutes when Dan, Jace, and, who I'm assuming is Frank, come out of the house with looks on their faces that make me glad it's not directed at me. The three of them come down the front stoop to meet me on the driveway, and I laugh at myself, wondering if the photographer is getting shots of this. They stop in front of me with varying degrees of rage on their face.

Jace is the first to speak, "Here's how this is going to go: he's shooting at my house, so I go with you and ask him to leave after he hands over the images. Frank, you'll record the whole thing for the police if it comes to that." He gives Frank a pointed look, "Do not egg him on. Got it?" Frank just shrugs, not giving us a real answer, and now I'm a little concerned about why Hope thought I should have him with me for this. Jace rolls his eyes at Frank and continues, "Dan, stay back a bit and be ready to call the police. I'm only going to ask him once before we call."

The three of them start walking toward the car without me, and I'm left a little stunned before I make my way over to catch up with them. I'm beginning to wonder if I need to be here at all. The guy is looking at the viewfinder on his camera, so he doesn't see us walk up. I lean forward and tap on his window, making him jump, then freeze when he sees who is standing next to his car. I make a gesture to roll down his window, and he cracks it enough for us to hear each other.

"I'm not going to introduce myself since I have a feeling you know who I am. I don't want your name, I don't care. All I need to know is who you're shooting for."

Jace chimes in then, "This is private property, and you were not invited. My friend here is recording this for everyone's safety." At that, Frank gives a little finger wave making me snort a laugh.

Turning back to the photographer, I cross my arms and wait for a reply. He holds up his hands in a placating gesture, "Dude, come on. You know I can't tell you that."

My anger flares at his callousness, "I am not your 'dude' nor your 'buddy', 'pal', or 'friend'. What I am, is pissed. You have followed me to a private residence and, I assume, taken images that were not consented to. This is what's going to happen: you're going to tell me who hired you to follow me; give me the camera, memory card, and any other method of storage you use—don't worry, you're also going to tell me where you work so I can have it all sent back to your office—then you're going to leave this property, and me, alone. Is that clear?"

The photographer sits there and seems to consider his options. While we've been talking, Dan has moved to lean against the hood of the guy's car and Frank has moved around to the back corner so he can presumably get a better angle of all of our faces. This guy has nowhere to go, and he's outnumbered if he wants to try to start something.

"Okay, fine. She said her name is Sandra. She paid me to follow you around for a few days and get some pictures. I don't know anything else about her though, I swear."

"Good, now the camera."

"I'll give you the memory cards and erase everything right here and now in front of you, but I'm not giving you my camera. This costs more than my phone."

"You'll give me every single memory card in your possession, hand over the camera for me to delete everything myself, and hand over your laptop for us to go through as well."

He starts to protest when Frank speaks up, "You've done well so far, kid. Don't fuck it up now. I'm not afraid to spend the night in jail. Are you?"

The photographer sighs and complies. Once we've gone through everything, I send him on his way with the instruction to have this woman contact my office Monday morning to set up a meeting. With that handled, we all head back to the house to enjoy the party.

***

Everything is going great. Cynthia and Dan have been so kind and accepting of me being in Hope and Lizzie's lives. We're sitting down around the table for cake and ice cream when Lizzie toddles over between me and Hope. Hope immediately backs her chair up so that Lizzie can sit in her lap, but she turns to me and says, "Up, daddy."

Everything stops.

I stiffly reach down to pick her up, placing her in my lap as I hold my breath.

Cynthia lets out a sniffle, and I start to apologize.

"I'm so sorry. She just started this today at the cemetery. Hope and I were going to talk tonight about how to tell her that I'm not..."

Cynthia cuts me off with a shake of her head, holding out her hand to stop me. Dan leans in, puts his head on his wife's shoulder and takes a shaky breath.

"It's okay, Landon." Cynthia starts, "We knew there was a chance something like this would happen. Doesn't make it easier, but we knew..." She chokes on a sob, and I'm doing my best to hold back my own tears. She finally gets herself under control, "Dan told me what you did for the girls this morning and we all watched what you did this afternoon to protect them. Thank you. Thank you for making sure she won't forget him. Thank you for taking care of them both the way my son would have." She can't stop the tears this time, and when I look around the table, everyone is crying.

Standing up, I place Lizzie in my chair and go over to Cynthia. I put my hand on her shoulder, lean down, and wrap her in a hug. While I'm there, I promise her that I will tell Lizzie about Matt every day. I even ask her for pictures and stories I can tell her, since I don't know anything about him. Nodding her head, she gives me a squeeze before she and Dan excuse themselves to the guest room.

I return to my seat, pick up the little girl who has quickly become mine, and give Hope a chaste kiss. Resting my forehead on hers, I whisper, "I love you."

CHAPTER 22

Hope

After Lizzie's birthday, Landon moved in. I asked him that night if he would consider it, and he didn't even hesitate before kissing me goodbye, heading to his house, and packing more of his clothes. He came back to the house with a goofy grin on his face and said he didn't need any of the big things. He just wanted to be with us. I did offer the guest room as an office, though, which he reluctantly took. Said he didn't want to take any room away from us, which is super sweet, but we never use the room anyway, so it doesn't matter.

Having him live with us is amazing. We spend our mornings taking turns making breakfast and entertaining Lizzie, and our nights wrapped up in each other. I've never had such explosive sex before. Not that Matt didn't know what he was doing or anything, but this is just different. Even when we're not playing in our roles, it's just as intense. The man is more attentive to me than I was to myself when it was just me! We've discovered we don't really like using condoms and decided to go without them since I'm on the pill.

The real estate firm is going through a big purchase right now, and he's been staying a bit later at the office this last week to try to keep on top of everything. It makes me nervous when he stays late, and I know that's a result of Matt's accident, but even knowing that doesn't make me feel better. After I told Landon about how I was feeling, he started using the home office after dinner. If he can't get home in time to eat with us, he calls me on his way home and stays on the line with me until I hear him pull up.

It's probably a bit over the top, but it makes me feel better. Plus, when we're done talking about our day, I start to tease him. He has a thirty-minute drive home from the office without traffic, so when we're having one of those late-night calls, I start telling him what I want him to do to me when he gets home, and sometimes what I'm doing to myself while I wait for him to get to me.

When he finally does make it home, the sex is mind-blowing.

The way he comes in, already stripped of his shoes, tie hanging from his hand. He looks ready to absolutely ravish me. I love it. I love seeing him lose that control he likes so much. The first time we did that, he came in with his shirt buttons popped and rolling across the hallway floors, his pants already undone.

Tonight, it'll be a little different.

Me: *image sent*

Landon: Jesus! James is sitting right here!

Landon: What else have you got?

I send him a few more images, each one becoming more revealing.

Landon: I'm on my way home.

Landon: Do not move.

Grinning to myself, I lay waiting for him.

Twenty-five minutes later, I hear the garage door open and close, then his shod feet on the hardwood.

He barrels into the room, "I fucking love you." Lunging for me, his mouth latches onto mine in a searing kiss. When he breaks for air, he dips his head to my breasts.

"Fucking love these tits," he growls before sucking a nipple into his mouth. He rolls the other between his thumb and forefinger, torturing both before swapping sides to continue. The hand that's not currently full of my nipple travels down my waist and dips between us, searching for my center. When he comes to the soaked spot, Landon pops off my breast with a deep, satisfied groan.

Looking at me, "You've been playing with Daddy's pussy, haven't you? Making sure you're good and ready to take my cock."

Throwing my head back as his fingers enter me, I let out a muffled groan of my own, trying not to wake Lizzie. "Fuck! Yes. I've been playing with my pussy, waiting for you. Please. Please fuck me, Daddy."

I'm bordering on delirious when I hear Landon's answering growl. The rumble is chest deep as he plunges forward, sinking his cock to the hilt. *When did he get naked?* The stretch around his massive size burns a bit, but he holds still to let me adjust for a minute before he loses his control completely.

He draws back slowly, the muscles in his neck tense and his pulse racing, giving short teasing, thrusts as he slides out before slamming back in. His pace is hard and fast, and I'm already building. I can feel it coming, but so can he. He slows his pace down, taking his time to grind his hips down on my needy little clit. He looks into my eyes each time he does, and I tighten around him a little more.

Landon stops his thrusting to pull a pillow from behind me and puts it under my hips, changing the angle. With this new angle, he's hitting my G-spot over and over again. It's too much.

So when he decides to suck a nipple into his mouth, I fly over the edge. Landon fucks me through the aftershocks and starts all over.

Dragging me back up that cliff.

He flips us over, putting me on top, "Ride me, baby girl. Fuck yourself on Daddy's cock. Take what you want."

So, I do. I raise up, far enough that only his swollen head is left, then drop down hard. Over and over, before I lean forward to take his mouth with mine while I grind my clit onto his base. His breathing is growing ragged, and I know he's getting close. Leaning back, I put my hands on his thighs, bracing myself. From this angle, he can watch my tits bounce, and I know he loves it when he reaches out to grab their weight. He can only stand not being in control for long, and suddenly he's rolling us back over. Pulling out, he flips me on my stomach before I can protest and lifts my hips up and back, impaling me on his awaiting cock.

He loses himself in me. No longer able to hold a rhythm and keeping a furious pace, he fucks me until I can feel the onslaught coming again. When I start to tighten around him, he reaches one hand around my hips and gives my clit the perfect amount of pressure while rubbing tight circles around it.

I detonate.

I fall forward into the pillows on a scream, and then I feel Landon tense behind me. My orgasm dragging his to the surface. He comes with a strangled roar, burying himself as far as he can get as he fills me. He sags forward, hardly able to hold himself up. Rolling to the side, he brings me with him. Our naked bodies tangled, and our breaths coming in choppy as we come back to ourselves.

"I love you, Hope."

"I love you, too, Landon."

And with that, we both fall into a blissful sleep.

The next morning passes in a blur. Landon and I get Lizzie fed, dressed, and out the door for school before heading off to work. When I get settled at my desk, I start going through my emails and the schedules for both Landon and James. As I'm working, I notice an interview request comes in. It's the same magazine that Landon interviewed with when Reed Enterprises first started to take off. The subject line reads *Follow Up Piece*, so I forward it to Landon for him to make the decision about accepting or not, and move on with the rest of my day.

Around lunch, Landon replies, telling me to accept the interview and add it to his calendar for Friday morning. The magazine accepts the proposed time and says a woman named Sandra will stop by at nine Friday morning to conduct the interview. Sending all the details over to Landon and adding it to his Friday schedule takes no time at all. I don't expect him to show up to my office after everything has been finalized, but here he is barreling in like a bat out of hell.

"Cancel the interview."

I don't really appreciate the way he's speaking to me, so I decide to correct his approach. Doing my best impression I say, "Hey, baby girl! I hope you've had a great morning so far! Thank you for working so hard, we really appreciate everything you've done for us since you've started. That said, do you think you could do me a huge favor and cancel the interview scheduled for Friday?"

Switching back to my own voice, "Hey, Landon! I have had a great morning so far, and I'd be happy to contact the magazine and ask about a reschedule or cancellation. Could you give me a reason for it though? They seemed rather eager to speak with you."

While I found the whole bit hilarious, Landon does not look amused. He narrows his eyes at me and steps into the office, closing the door behind him.

Shit.

I'm in trouble.

"Thought that was funny, did you?"

"A little bit, yeah. Now before you go all *Daddy* on me, will you tell me why I'm canceling this interview? I think it would be a great way to generate more business by getting the company back in the public eye with an update on the agency's success."

Landon plops down in the chair in front of my desk, leans back, and just stares at me for a solid minute before he speaks again. When he does, I wish he hadn't.

"Sandra is the woman who did my last interview. She came onto me and when I turned her down, she got pretty mad about it. I never told you because; A. I didn't want to worry or upset you and B. I couldn't even remember her name, until reading it jogged my memory. The photographer that we saw outside of the house on Lizzie's birthday had apparently been following me around. I told him to tell the woman who was paying him to schedule an appointment with me on Monday morning so we could talk. I never had a meeting scheduled for that day and I have no proof, but it feels too coincidental that the person paying a photographer to stalk me is also named Sandra."

Raising my hands in front of me, "Hold on. Let me get this straight. You think this magazine reporter is having you followed and you never thought to inform me about it? Did you consider how this would impact my life? My daughter's life? Do you think this is the person who's been leaving those things at our houses?" With each question, my voice gets louder.

How dare he withhold this information! This could put Lizzie at risk!

My indignation is short-lived when a thought crosses my mind and my blood runs cold at the thought. My hands grow cold and I can feel the blood leave my face.

Landon is beside me in a heartbeat, "Hope! What's wrong? Talk to me!"

"The cemetery." Those words are the only ones I can get out at the moment. I can see Landon's panic starting to climb as he holds my face in his hands, begging me to tell him what's going on. Taking a breath, I tell him what I saw at the cemetery as I was leaving. About the woman on the ground sobbing hysterically and how I now think the flash I saw may have been a camera lens reflecting the light.

Someone could have pictures of my daughter. That thought nearly sends me hyperventilating.

At some point during my panic, Landon must have called Diana into the office. He goes over everything that's happened with her while I sit in a stupor. As he finishes retelling his account of events and his working theory, Diana is visibly angry.

"Landon Reed! You should have come to me as soon as she left the first time! I should have documentation of this little stunt!" She stops for a moment to compose herself before continuing. "Sorry, I shouldn't have raised my voice when you're both already stressed. Hope, talk to me. You've hardly blinked."

I can't focus on anything in particular, so I just stare at my desk as I speak.

"At the cemetery, as I was leaving, I saw something reflective flash in the sunlight...or maybe it was actually a camera flash, I don't know, but Lizzie was with us." *There could be pictures of my daughter floating around somewhere, anywhere. They could do anything with those images.* "Landon..." I can't finish my thought, I'm so worried about someone following me and Lizzie around, with us completely unaware.

He makes sure I'm looking into his eyes when he tells me, "I'll take care of it, baby girl. I swear to you." He's so sure, I actually believe him.

Diana clears her throat to get our attention. "I'm not sure if he told you or not, but James ordered a new security system last month from a new private security firm. It's being installed right now. The standard package comes with enough cameras to cover the main office, the front door of the suite, and the conference room. All in all, we're looking at five cameras spread throughout the office common areas. Jamie down in the security office can go over the specifics with you later. Hold the interview in the conference room. Because there will be recording devices, we have to place a sign by the front door informing visitors that they're being recorded...but we don't have to point that sign out...just saying."

Landon gets a gleam in his eye that would scare me if I were on the receiving end.

"Hope, keep the interview as planned."

"What?! You want to meet with the crazy chick who can't take rejection?!"

"No, baby girl. I want to set up the crazy chick to have evidence of her attempted indiscretions so we can send it over to her magazine. If that doesn't get her to leave us alone, I'll go to the police and file a restraining order. We'll let the chips fall where they may after that."

"Landon, if this is her doing, antagonizing her doesn't seem like the best idea."

"You're probably right, baby, but we need her to back off, if it is her. At the very least, she'll get in trouble for sexual harassment in the workplace."

I sigh in resignation. I can see there's no changing his mind.

"Di, I want it on record that I am passionately against this plan and protest it vehemently."

"Noted and documented." Turning to Landon, "I'm with her on this, Landon. It's a bad idea." With that, she walks out the door, softly shutting it behind her.

CHAPTER 23
Landon

Friday Morning

It's almost time for the interview. I'm actually a little anxious waiting for Sandra to show up so we can get what I imagine is a sham of an interview over with. At 9:00 a.m., I'm sitting in the conference room, going through some emails, when Hope escorts Sandra into the room.

I can't help but rake my eyes over Hope, taking her in. She looks absolutely stunning in her black slacks and ivory blouse. The flush in her cheeks left over from this morning's orgasm added the perfect touch to her already delicious appearance. I also note a tense set to her shoulders that wasn't there an hour ago. *Something I've spent ample time preventing.*

I slide my eyes from my girl to look at the woman standing next to her and I'm a bit taken aback at the open hostility in her eyes and the fact that I recognize her from the restaurant from my first date with Hope. She's glaring at Hope with a look that would make a lesser person shrivel up and wither away making my back go up as every protective instinct I have rears its head.

Time to get Hope out of here.

"Thank you, Hope. I'll take it from here, please leave the door open when you leave."

After Hope is gone, Sandra's eyes soften as if she didn't look like she was plotting my girl's demise thirty seconds ago.

She steps forward as if to give me a hug and I sidestep. There's a flash of anger across her face before she clears it, "Landon, it's so good to see you! How have you been? I see the company has been doing well. What have you been up to?"

I hold my hand out for a shake, "Hello, Sandra. I thought you were a reporter. At least, that's what one usually assumes when an interview gets published in a magazine. How come you were working at the restaurant's hostess stand a few months back?"

"I freelance. I write as I please and companies hire me to do work for them when they need me."

I narrow my eyes and take a seat, steering the direction of this meeting away from the personal. "Very well. What questions did you have lined up for me today?"

Aside from a disgruntled look at my dismissal, she moves on to the questions she needs answered for her article. By the time things start wrapping up, I begin to wonder if I was projecting my unease onto her. That is until she leans closer, causing her shirt to gape open at the top and reveal the dip between her breasts. With a sly grin, she lowers the tone of her voice in what I imagine is an attempt at seduction.

"One last question, Landon. Where are we going for drinks after this?" As she talks, she slides her hand closer to mine and tries to intertwine our fingers. Having none of that, I push to stand.

"Thank you for coming out today. I'm looking forward to seeing your article. I hope you have a wonderful rest of your day." I try to get to the door, but Sandra steps in my path and blocks the way. Raising her hand to my chest, she starts to run her fingers up toward my collar. I step back, my blood pressure rising at the blatant disrespect from this woman.

"You don't have to pretend anymore, Landon. After this article goes live, we can start seeing each other in the open. I know you feel the connection between us. Didn't you like the rose I sent?"

My blood freezes. *She is the one sending flowers to the office?*

She reaches forward as if to touch me again and I back up, putting the table between us. "That's quite enough, Sandra. We're done here. Leave."

She gets a manic looking gleam in her eyes and her brows draw together. "You know, it's not nice to ignore me, Landon. You don't need that pig clinging to you when you have me."

"I'm not going to repeat myself again. You need to leave. And you need to have some respect for my staff. I will not tolerate anyone belittling the people in my employ, let alone someone I'm dating."

She releases an unholy sound that borders on a screech as she makes a move to come closer. Before she can take another step toward me, James walks in. "Excuse me, sorry to interrupt. Landon, I need you in my office. Something has come up with the Aurther contract."

Leaning over the table and speaking low I tell her, "Don't you ever disrespect my woman again." I stand back to my full height before I dismiss her, "Thank you for your time, Sandra. Excuse me." Thankfully, she lets me pass, but not without a parting remark.

"This isn't over, Landon. You love me. I know you do."

With that hanging in the air, James and I go to his office where Diana is sitting at his desk doing something on the computer.

"Where's Hope?" I need her with me, with no chance of running into that viper disguised as a woman.

Diana continues typing on the keyboard, barely glancing up so James chimes in.

"I told her to stay in her office until one of us comes to get her. Diana told me about your theory, so we decided to watch the interview on the new system, as the clips were recorded and saved. Di is compiling all the clips from the time she entered the conference room to the time I stepped in and is sending them to the magazine's chief editor."

Turning to Diana I ask, "Is Sandra gone?"

A few more taps on the keyboard and Diana nods her head in confirmation. That's all I need before I take off for Hope's office.

Her door is locked when I get there, so I knock and call out to her. She has the door thrown open before I can finish telling her it's me and she practically tackles me to the ground in a hug.

"Don't you ever do something so stupid again. That could've gone completely off the rails! What if she had a weapon? Did you think about that? I'm so angry with you, damn it!"

My sweet girl, she's practically shaking in fear and anger. To be honest, I'm a little shaken myself, but I walk us further into her office, close the door, and sit on the floor with her in my lap. We sit like that for a few minutes until we settle. When her breathing evens out, I grab her chin and bring her eyes to mine.

"Never again, baby girl. Never again." I seal my promise with a deep, seeking kiss. I never want to see this level of fear on her face again. I can't imagine the state she would be in if something had actually happened. Once we gather ourselves up off the floor we head back to my office to find James leaning over Diana with a grin on his face.

This guy is completely under her spell, and he won't do anything about it.

I shake my head at myself and move Hope to the couch so we can find out what Diana has been doing that has James looking like the cat that got the canary.

"What have you been doing, D?"

"Oh, nothing really," the smirk on her face says otherwise, so I arch my brow and wait her out.

She huffs, "Fine. I'll tell you. Like James said earlier, I compiled all the interview clips and sent them to the magazine's editor-in-chief. What he didn't see is that I informed them that I would be sending everything to the police as well and that Sandra would be charged with criminal trespassing should she ever show up here again." Pausing, she looks at me, "You will be going down to the station when we finish this conversation and filing a personal restraining order for yourself, Hope, and Lizzie if need be. All the files are sitting in both your inboxes right now."

I sigh and relax into the back of the couch, pulling Hope closer to me. "Thank you, D. Whatever you need, it's yours. As for the station…" I release an exasperated breath. "I was going to head down there anyway. I think Sandra is the one who's been leaving notes and creepy 'gifts' around our houses." Hope tenses in my arms and James and Diana have expressions on their faces that would be funny in any other circumstance.

Then they both lose their ever-loving shit. They take turns yelling at us for not telling them and how irresponsible we've been to keep it to ourselves. Once they get it all out of their system, they settle and ask how they can help.

Looking at Hope as I speak, "Let's stick to the plan for now. Send the files to the magazine, go to the police, and live our life. Anything that happens from there, that's a different story."

CHAPTER 24

Landon

One Month Later

This purchase is going to be the death of me. That is, if the stress of waiting for something else to happen with the Sandra situation doesn't do me in first. I feel like we're sitting on pins and needles, just waiting for her to do something else. I'm quickly approaching my breaking point, and I know Hope is even closer than I am — especially after everything that went down in the office. There's no way she's done with us. In the meantime, James and I have been pulling extra hours at the office.

I'm tired of the late nights, the endless emails and negotiations, all of it. I just want to be at home with my girls. It's going on nine o'clock now. I've already missed dinner and bedtime with Lizzie, and I'm trying my damnedest to be home in time to go to bed with Hope. We've been working on purchasing an empty plot of land out in the country that's absolutely massive. I'm talking, big enough to either build a small neighborhood or make it two large estates.

Honestly, the location is gorgeous.

It's pretty far from the city, so noise is minimal, but it's close enough to a major area that whoever decides to purchase the house we build won't be too far from grocery stores, entertainment, and schools. I can imagine the property all finished now: Classic ranch-style home, but grander. I'm thinking five bedrooms. A large master suite with a sitting area and a guest suite, but leaving the other rooms basic to accommodate kids, more guests, or maybe an office. Open concept in the main living spaces with a large stone fireplace in the living room. A spacious kitchen, with white quartz countertops, matte black cabinets, and an island with a built-in dishwasher and extra cabinets. The yard would be massive. A large shed on the back of the property with a gated pool nearby for the kids to swim. Right off the back doors, would be a patio for an entertaining space and a fire pit off in the corner.

Yeah, that'd be perfect. And it would sell quickly in that particular buyer market.

I finally reach a stopping point after sending one last email to James with the contract for the property attached, and decide to head home. There shouldn't be much traffic tonight, so it shouldn't take me long. I call Hope when I get to the parking garage, but she doesn't answer. *Damn, maybe she's already asleep.* Putting the phone down and starting the car, I make my way to the exit. Turning on my blinker, I look around and don't see anyone coming, so I start to pull out. I'm already halfway out of the garage before I see the other car, and I try to speed up to get out of the way, but they're going too fast.

There's a deafening crunch, the smell of gunpowder, and then everything gets a little fuzzy. I look around to orient myself and try to shake the daze, my airbags deployed, which is probably the gunpowder I smell, and my car is totaled; I don't even need to look at it to know. I try reaching for the door, but I can't move my arm. I look down and see it doesn't look right, and it hurts like a bitch to try to move. Looking out my window, I can see the other car, but not the driver. *Did they run off?* Someone is nearby though and already talking on the phone. He looks over at me and asks me through the window, "Hey man, are you alright?"

My head is pounding when I give him a stiff nod. *Damn, that hurts.*

"Can you get out? I called 911, they should be here soon."

"No," I croak. "My door is jammed. I think my arm is broken or something, and my head is pounding." I'm not sure he can even hear me, but at the very least he's gathered that I can't get out of the car.

Yanking on my door to force it open, "Okay, just stay there. Is there anyone you need to call?"

Shit. Hope is gonna freak out.

Where did my phone go?

"My wife. I need to call my wife." I sweep my eyes around in an attempt to reduce the pounding in my skull, "I can't find my phone."

I belatedly realize what I said and can't bring myself to correct it. *She'll be my wife soon enough.*

"Okay, I'll call her for you. What's her number?"

I try to rattle it off, but I'm just so tired. Any adrenaline that may have been running through my system fades and the exhaustion from work and the accident sets in and I start to fall asleep when the sound of sirens pulls closer. The guy beside me tries to get me to read off her number, but I just want to sleep.

"I'll call her when I wake up. Hope…" I trail off as darkness closes in.

***

My eyes are heavy, and there's a harsh light that peeks through when I try to open them. My mind starts to run away from me as I come back around. *I need Hope.* I need to call her and tell her I was in an accident, but that I'll be okay.

At least, I assume I'll be okay.

Phone. Where's my phone?

I start to blindly reach around looking for it when I run into wires. Confused, I force my eyes to open and look around the room. There's a nurse beside me checking machines when I turn my head. I try to clear the sleep from my voice and reach for her when I say,

"Hope. I need Hope. Where is she?"

The nurse startles. "Oh! Heavens, you scared me. I'm glad to see you're awake! You gave us a scare for a minute when you passed out."

"Where's my phone? I need to call my wife." *Yeah, I like the sound of that. Gonna make that happen soon.*

"Here it is!" She hands it to me, "The gentleman who called 911 found it and stuck it in your pocket when they were loading you into the ambulance. The good news is there's no major trauma to your head. The bad news is that your radius was fractured in the crash, and a few ribs were broken. We sent you to get imaged to make sure there wasn't a risk to any internal organs and checked for any bleeding, but you were all good. The arm will take some time to heal, and I'll give you instructions on when to see the doctor for follow-up X-rays when you get discharged..."

I barely hear her; all I can think about is Hope.

As if my thoughts conjured the angel herself, she rushes into the room with frantic eyes and tear-stained cheeks.

CHAPTER 25

Hope

It was like reliving the night Matt died all over again.

I had gone to take a shower and didn't bring my phone to the bathroom with me. When I came back, I saw a missed call from Landon, so I called him back. Only it wasn't Landon that picked up.

"Uh, hello?"

"Who is this? Where's Landon?"

"Please tell me you're his wife? I've been trying to call her, but he passed out before I could get a name."

"My name is Hope! Where's Landon?! What the hell happened? Who are you?"

"Hope! That's what he was muttering about. Well, I witnessed an accident your husband was in. He's being loaded into the ambulance right now, but he was conscious when I called so I was able to speak to him a bit. Let me hand the phone to the paramedic so you can get the details."

I'm shaking. I can't breathe. Landon was in an accident? He's being loaded into an ambulance?

"Ma'am? Are you there?" The tone of the voice on the other end of the line suggests that he's been trying to get my attention for a minute.

"Yes, I'm here. My name is Hope Reed. My husband, Landon, is he okay?"

"I can't disclose this sort of information over the phone, I'm sorry. I can tell you which hospital we're going to, though."

After I get the name of the hospital, I call my parents in hysterics and ask them to come over to sit with Lizzie. When they get to the house, I can't stop shaking enough to hold my keys, so my mom drives me to the hospital. On the way there, I keep going over the worst-case scenarios. They play on a loop like some sort of horror film that only I can see.

When we pull up, my mom walks me to the information desk so I can figure out what's going on.

"Landon Reed. Please tell me what room Landon Reed is in."

"Are you a spouse or family?"

I start to tell the woman I'm his girlfriend when my mother steps in. "She's his wife."

"May I see your ID?"

Shit. This isn't gonna work. Since Landon moved, our addresses match, but our names don't.

Thank God for moms. "They just got married last week. They took a short vacation away from their daughter and got back two days ago."

The woman starts to protest, and I collapse.

Sobbing hysterically, I beg her, "Please. Please let me see him. I can't lose him. Our daughter, she's three. Please tell me where her daddy is."

Body shaking sobs tear through me and I feel sick. The woman's expression softens, and she nods telling us the room number.

I walk to the elevator bank, numb to the feel of my feet on the floor and the button under my fingers, with my mama following behind me just in case. When we get to Landon's room, I can't bring myself to open his door. All the dark thoughts from before come rushing back, and I stand rooted to the spot. My mother touches my shoulder, jolting me back to the real world. She turns me to face her and tells me, "Listen to me. He will be fine. This isn't the ICU. It's a basic emergency room. Go in there and see for yourself. I can hear him talking right now. He. Is. Fine."

I nod in response and turn the handle, peeking in to ease myself into what I'm about to see, and all but falling into the room when I do see him.

The relief I feel is so all-consuming that I can feel my knees weaken to the point that I need to lean on the door for support. He's sitting up, phone in hand, and humming along as the nurse runs through what all happened and his diagnosis. He looks up at me when the door opens and smiles through the discomfort he's clearly in.

"Hey, baby girl. I was just about to call you. I'm so sorry. So, so sorry. The other car came out of nowhere."

I hold up my hand to halt his apologies. He doesn't have anything to apologize to me about. Turning to the nurse, I address her.

"I apologize for the way my husband has ignored the rundown you've so kindly been giving him." I turn my glare on Landon, and his mouth is hanging open in shock, whether at the anger radiating through my tone or the fact that I called him my husband, I don't know. Frankly, I don't care right now.

"Would you mind telling me what's going on and how I can care for him when he comes home?"

She stifles a laugh and repeats what she was telling Landon before I came in. As I sit on the edge of his bed listening to the nurse, I rest my hand on his leg, needing some sort of connection to ground me. After she finishes, she leaves the room, and I look to Landon, who is smirking at me.

"What the hell could possibly be funny at a time like this? I was so scared! I called you back, and someone else answered and told me he had witnessed an accident and found you in one of the cars! Damnit Landon! You have to be more careful! I can't lose you! I won't survive it! You–"

He cuts me off when he reaches for me with his good arm and pulls me into a searing kiss. "I'm sorry, baby girl. I love you too."

I start sobbing again, bowing my head to his chest as my shoulders collapse from the strain they've been under the last two hours. He gently strokes my hair and murmurs soothing words to me until I regain my composure. After I settle, he lifts my face to his with his finger and holds my head hostage by my chin.

"I love you so much, baby girl. Matt told me you would be a guiding light in my life and that I should give you the world. I plan to do just that, because you are the most perfect woman I have ever met. And your daughter has wormed her way into my heart so deeply I don't know where she ends and I begin. This isn't how I wanted to do this, and I don't have a ring, I was going to go look later in the week. But I want you to be my wife. Hearing you call me your husband was a dream come true, and I want it to be a reality. If you don't want to change your name, that's fine. I just want you to be mine. So, Hope Marie Lawson, will you marry me?"

I sit stunned for a moment before I sob out a choked "Yes!" Wiping my tears, "Yes! Yes, I'll marry you! And I'll change my name. I may not change Lizzie's, but I will change mine. I belong to you and I don't want anyone to mistake that."

After sitting together on his hospital bed for a while in comfortable silence, I turn to look at him.

"You asked my dad for permission, right?"

Before he can respond, my mom comes in with tears coming down her face and a smile on her face.

"He sure did. At Lizzie's birthday forever ago! I've been waiting ages to get a call from you!"

We both laugh. Well, I laugh. Landon groans when he tries because of his ribs.

"I'm sorry to have kept you waiting, Maria." With a nod in my direction, "I was giving this one time to catch up with me."

"Hey! Who said I wasn't already there?"

Mom eventually says her goodbyes, and we settle in for the night. It'll be a long recovery, but we'll be okay. With a self-satisfied smile, I think; *I'll be the best nurse he's ever had.*

Landon

Hope and I are sitting in my hospital room when the cops show up. They came to take my statement about the accident and they ask me all the standard questions:

"Can you describe the accident?"

"Are you able to describe the vehicle that hit you?"

"Did you see the other driver?"

When I tell them I didn't see anything, they nod along without much other response. They let me know that they spoke with the guy who called 911 for me, and he only saw that the person who took off was small in stature, and whoever it was ran off immediately after hitting me.

Hope sits with me on the bed, her hand tightly grasping mine. She's tense and worried. Her body is so tightly wound that one more thing might just shatter her. The officers inform me that they'll make their report and that I should have my insurance company contact the precinct for the case number. When they have all the information they need, they leave me with a contact card and a "get well soon" then Hope and I are alone again.

"I still can't believe someone hit you and took off like that."

I stroke my thumb across hers, "I can't either. I'm so sorry to have scared you the way I did. I shouldn't've left so late."

"Landon, please don't apologize for someone else's mistake. You were working. It's not like you were out and about partying it up. It was an accident. I'm just glad you're okay."

Regardless of what she says, it will likely be a while before I work late at the office again. My arm is killing me, and my head hurts from the whiplash I'm sure I have from the impact. *I'll be going to the chiropractor as soon as I'm out of here.*

"Come here, baby girl." She doesn't hesitate to cuddle closer to me. I pull her in on my good side and we lie in the bed in comfortable silence for a while, our breaths synchronizing and slowing. Eventually, we fall asleep wrapped in each other, taking a moment of peace.

CHAPTER 26

Hope

We finally get discharged the next afternoon, and I call my mom to come pick us up from the hospital. I haven't been that scared in a long time. Seeing Landon lying in the hospital bed, awake and alert, only took the edge off. I feel like I'm on the verge of shattering, and I'm not sure how much more I can take. Landon is in a cast, and he keeps rotating his neck like it's stiff. I can't believe this happened. I don't even know how to process all of this. *Who would run away after an accident??* Turning to Landon, I scan him over, as if more injuries will have appeared since we were discharged.

"Are you okay? Are you in any pain?"

"Baby, I'm okay. I promise. I've taken the dose of pain meds, and I'm comfortable. I'll be glad to get home and be with my girls. How is Lizzie?"

Sighing in relief, I lean into his good shoulder just to be closer to him. "She's okay. She's worried about you and will likely be clingy when we get home, but other than that, she's fine."

He leans his head back and inhales deeply, releasing it in a slow breath. "Good. That's good. I don't want to worry her."

Leveling a look at him, "Well, you've worried us both, regardless of what you want. We're just glad that you're okay."

Truth is, Lizzie was pretty frantic when she woke up without me at the house. I ended up staying at the hospital despite visiting hours ending an hour before Landon was hit. My mom video called me this morning, and when I answered, my sweet Lizzie had tears running down her cheeks and was all frantic about why I wasn't there this morning to make breakfast. We finally pull up to the house, and Lizzie is out on the front porch before we even put the car in park.

"Daddy! Where you go?? That a boo-boo?"

Landon gets down on his knees on the driveway and holds his good arm out to grab Lizzie as she throws herself into him.

"Hey baby, I missed you so much. I was in a car accident and had to stay in the hospital last night. Mommy came to keep me company, but I'm home now and I'm okay. I'm home now."

Watching them together makes my heart beat harder in my chest. I can't believe how lucky I am to have met him that night at the bar. I wasn't looking for anything other than the girl's night I went out for, but here we are. And I couldn't be happier.

"Come on, Lizzie Bear. Let's get daddy set up in bed to rest, and we can cook up something yummy for him while he naps."

Lizzie turns her bright blue eyes to me and gasps in excitement. "Mama cook?"

Smiling, I nod. "Yes, baby. Let's go on in."

She turns and races up the front steps, stopping long enough to holler back at us to hurry up. She loves cooking with me just as much as I love her joining me in the kitchen. Landon and I head in, and I shoo him off to the couch. He tries to fight me on it until he sees the glower I send his way, after which he relents and heads over to the living room. Lizzie and I spend most of the afternoon cooking up a storm and even bake a batch of cookies to munch on after dinner.

The evening passes in a pleasant blur of giggles and cuddles, and I don't think I've been this happy in a long time. Lizzie falls asleep sprawled across our laps while we're watching a Disney movie, and I eventually move her up to her bed. I make Landon move to our room while I'm putting Lizzie down, and by the time I make it back, he's fast asleep. I lean against the door and give myself a second to savor his sleep filled expression. His strong features that have been so stress-filled as of late are relaxed in sleep, giving him a softer look. Closing the door behind me, I head back downstairs to turn off the lights and television when I hear a light tapping on the back window, almost like the brushing of a tree limb against glass in a storm. *I guess it's going to rain tonight.*

I brush off the noise and finish turning everything off before heading up to bed.

***

The sound of shattering glass wakes us from a dead sleep. Landon tries to keep me in the bed, but he grunts in pain and can't keep me. I lurch up and over to the bedside table for the .9mm I keep locked up and move toward the hallway. I stop off in Lizzie's room to move her to the bed with Landon before heading down the stairs.

Wrong house, motherfucker.

Growing up in the south means that I'm plenty familiar with guns and my dad made sure that I know how to use one. I may not be tactically trained, and I may not be super intimidating to look at, but for all intents and purposes, they just threatened my daughter, and there is nothing I wouldn't do to protect her. Easing down the stairs, I keep the barrel of the gun angled down and my finger resting on the trigger guard.

I peak around the corner and slowly move my gaze across the space, not seeing anything out of place other than the shattered window next to the backdoor. After checking over the space, I go back up the stairs to the bedroom and grab my phone to call the police.

Landon and I share a look, but don't say a word.

The police show up shortly after I hang up with dispatch, and we run through what we know. They check the surrounding area to see if they can find anything, but other than some matted-down grass, there's nothing. It's disappointing, but honestly not unexpected. They come back around the front of the house, where Landon and I meet them on the front porch. Lizzie stayed asleep for the most part, she was groggy when I woke her up to move her to my bed but managed to doze back off once she snuggled up to Landon. The police knocking on the door woke her up though and she's been anxious ever since, clinging to Landon like a spider monkey. I don't blame her. The adrenaline that crashed through my system when I heard the glass shatter is wearing off, and I feel like I'm going to drop at any second. The police are still here asking questions, and I'm only half listening to Landon as he speaks.

"Do either of you have any enemies you can think of?"

"Enemies?!" I blurt out. "Why would either of us have any enemies? He's in real estate, and I only just started working again a few months ago!"

"I know it seems crazy, Ms. Lawson, but if you can think of anything out of the ordinary that may have happened recently it could be helpful. If it were the front window, I'd chalk it up to bored teenagers and run-of-the-mill vandalism, but you have a locked gate surrounding the backyard and a privacy fence. That, to me, shows a level of determination that you wouldn't see if it were teenagers looking for a quick getaway."

At that, I can feel the blood drain from my face as I look at Landon. He wears a grim expression that tells me he's thinking the same thing as me.

Turning to the officers, he tells them, "We've had some issues with a journalist lately. She interviewed me a few years ago when my company was just taking off, and we had a follow up about a month ago. She came onto me and refused to back down when I rejected her advances." Landon adjusts Lizzie in his hold, and I reach for her to give his good arm a break. He passes her over as he speaks. "We have cameras in the conference room for security purposes and sent the recordings to the police and her magazine when we filed a restraining order. She's the only person I can think of that would have a reason to retaliate."

"Okay, can you provide her information?"

"Her personal information? No sir, but I can give you the name of the magazine and see if they could provide any information you may need."

The officer nods, "That works. Thank you." He turns to me, "I'm sorry you guys had to go through this tonight. We'll get out of your hair and let you know if we need any other details."

All I can do is nod and hold Lizzie a little tighter. I'm ready to crawl back in bed and forget this night ever happened.

CHAPTER 27
Landon

Two Weeks Later

I am beyond ready to get this fucking cast off. It's so damn bulky, and I keep bumping it into stuff, not to mention how irritating it is to not be able to scratch the itch underneath; that has done nothing but drive me absolutely insane with a rage I've never felt before.

I just need to scratch!

Hope thinks it's damn funny to see me struggle like this. I believe her exact words were, "It makes you seem more real, less put together."

As if this pain-in-the-ass thing would get in the way of punishing her. *Ha!* I showed her real quick that I don't need two hands to have her begging for Daddy.

She still thinks it's amusing.

I've taken the last two weeks to work from home where I can, relying more on James than I normally do. I enjoyed it the first week, but I'm over it now. I don't see how people work from home on a daily basis. I go from my bed to my office to my desk without leaving the house, and I'm going stir crazy. All my meetings have either been rescheduled, handed over, or conducted over video calls, and I'm ready to go back to the office.

I plan on heading in tomorrow and doing what I can before the pain gets too bad.

I might be ready for the cast to go, but I'm not stupid enough to overdo it and prolong my torture.

There's a knock on the front door around noon while I'm heating up leftovers from last night for lunch. I go to answer it and am stunned silent at the sight in front of me. Sandra is standing on the front porch with a glazed look in her eyes and appears to have some bruising across her collarbone.

"Sandra...what are you doing here? You need to leave."

"I came to check on you. I heard about the accident. Oh my, look at your arm! Are you okay?"

She reaches out as if to touch me, and I pull back.

"I'm fine. Thank you. Now it's time for you to go. I don't know how you heard about the accident, but I've had enough. Leave me alone."

At that, her entire demeanor shifts.

"Fine. I'll leave."

I close the door, double-check the lock, and head back to my office. About an hour later, I'm sitting in my chair when I get a notification on my computer. Switching screens, I see an email sitting in my inbox. Hope usually filters my inbox, so it's rare that I get an email that she hasn't already moved. Clicking it open, I read it:

Landon,

I'm sorry. I tried to make it painless. Don't worry, I'll take care of everything the right way this time.

- Yours

That's...odd...

It doesn't appear to be spam, so I click on the attachments. My pulse pounds harder when it opens to images of my car immediately after the accident. The picture is taken from the inside of another vehicle. You can see me through the driver's side window and the guy who helped me out. I close out the attachment and check the sender: *unknown@me.com*.

Fuck. That's not helpful.

Opening the attachments again, I look for anything that might tell me who the sender is, but it's not like I do this kind of thing for a living. I have no earthly idea what I'm even looking for other than...what? An accidental selfie? Like, *here's this threatening email with a picture of my face attached to it.* Unfortunately, I don't think anyone is that stupid. I scroll to the bottom of the image and see a second has been stitched in. My blood runs cold when I see a picture of Hope sitting in the office...wearing the outfit she left in this morning. Panicking, I reach for my phone to call Hope, only to see it light up with her name.

Sighing in relief, I answer, "Hey baby girl, I was—"

"Landon!" She sounds utterly panicked, and instantly I'm up and headed to the car.

"Hope? What's going on?"

"I don't know! Something is happening at the office; there's screaming and running, and I don't know what to do! I'm freaking the fuck out here!"

My body is moving on autopilot, grabbing my keys and wallet and walking out the door.

"I'm on my way. Unless you smell smoke, go to my office, lock the door, call the police, and hide in the bathroom.

Whatever you do, do not hang up with me. I'll be there as soon as I can."

"Landon," I hate that I can hear the panic in her voice, "what the hell is going on?"

"I don't know, baby. I haven't gotten any notifications from my security system. Once you call the police, hit the panic button on the underside of my desk. The silent alarm will go off and notify security, if they don't already know."

"Okay, I'm in your office." I can hear her panting breaths and the click of the lock. Something thuds lightly and I hear her moving my chair away from the desk to get to the phone. She's waiting for the dispatcher to answer when there's a heavy bang, and Hope lets out a startled gasp.

"What was that?!"

No answer.

"Hope?! Answer me! What was that noise!"

This time, I can hear whispering on her end before the line disconnects. Fresh panic surges through my system, and it's taking every ounce of restraint I possess not to throw my phone out the window. I'm so close to breaking every traffic law there is in order to get there faster. It feels like hours or *days* pass before I get a text.

Hope: Someone is trying to get into your office. I called the police, units are on their way. I'm hiding in the bathroom and don't want to make any noise.

I blow out a breath as a modicum of relief trickles in knowing she's okay. Using voice-to-text, I reply:

Me: Call me. You don't have to say anything, just stay on the line with me.

Her reply is instant.

Hope: Okay.

Her call comes through, and I start talking to her.

"Alright, baby girl. You're doing such a good job for me. Thank you for calling me back. I know it's scary right now, but everything will be okay. I'm almost to the office. When I get there, I'm going to come up for you and we're going to work our way out of this mess."

I don't want to tell her that Sandra showed up at the house, not right now, at least. I have a feeling her prints are all over what's happening right now. As if to prove my point, I hear knocking on the bathroom door, and a faint voice floats through the barrier.

FUCK!

I no longer care about traffic laws. I floor it, run the red light, and haul ass to my girl.

CHAPTER 28

Hope

I'm not sure I've ever been so scared in all my life. I have no idea what's happening in the building. I didn't smell any smoke, so I booked it to Landon's office. Diana had the day off, and James is out on a consultation; I'm completely on my own up here. Halfway through giving the police dispatch our information, there was a bang against the office door. I left the phone off the cradle, grabbed my cell, and scurried to the bathroom.

I don't think I've ever scurried in my life.

This is so not the time for amusing thoughts.

I'm huddled as far from the bathroom door as I can get when I hear another knock, this one much closer, followed by a voice that has made a guest appearance in my nightmares as of late.

"You can come out here and we can chat, or I can break down this door, and things will get much harder for us both."

Like hell am I moving.

"If you'd prefer, I can head to Lizzie's school. It's so precious looking, and she's just the sweetest little girl." She lets out a hysterical giggle before adding, "Wasn't it so funny that she called Landon 'daddy' at the graveyard?" More laughter, "And the look on your face! You looked like you'd been punched in the gut," her tone dipped to something dangerous, "and then, when you told him, you both looked so fucking thrilled. I wanted to pop out then, but I stayed hidden, only for you to notice me and offer me *comfort*." She spit the last word like it was poison. "As if you haven't had it out for me the entire time. How could you not recognize me?! You come along and take Landon from me and don't even have the decency to acknowledge the woman you pushed out?"

She's clearly lost her mind, but I only half heard what she said after she threatened my daughter. Gritting my teeth, I stand and pull my phone closer to my mouth so he can hear me.

"She just threatened Lizzie. I love you. I was going to sit and wait, but she pushed the wrong fucking button."

I don't wait to hear him reply, I just shove my phone in my back pocket and square my shoulders.

No one threatens my daughter.

As quietly as I can, I move to the door. It opens into the bathroom, so I ball my fingers into a fist and slowly–achingly slowly–I turn the lock. As soon as it clicks, I fling the door open and swing.

Despite the throbbing in my hand, there's a satisfying thud when her head reels back and she staggers away from the door. I don't even think before I throw myself at her. *How dare she threaten my daughter?!* I've never been in a fight before–I didn't realize how exhausting it actually is–but I can feel the adrenaline singing in my blood giving me the extra push I need to lay this bitch out. Can't say I ever pictured myself getting in a fight. I'm a mother for fuck's sake. But here I am going after another person like a rabid animal. Honestly, it's her own fucking fault. I can handle a lot, but I won't tolerate someone coming after my child.

Time doesn't seem to be moving at a normal pace. With the adrenaline rush, I feel like I can hear color and see sound; that's how crystal clear my focus is. I find myself straddling Sandra's chest and grabbing her wrists to try and hold her down, but she's writhing like a worm on a hook, and I can't keep my grip. She's able to shove me off her and the next thing I know, I'm looking at the pointy end of a blade. My first thought is, *at least it's not a gun*, and if that doesn't show how tired I am of this whole thing then nothing else will. My second thought is whether or not the police are still on the office line.

Slowly, I raise my hands and start moving backward. Sandra takes her time inching closer to me, knife aimed at my chest.

I'm just level with the corner of the desk when she demands, "Stop fucking moving."

I freeze, not wanting to risk pissing her off more than I already have. She's already sporting a swollen cheek, and I gotta say I'm a little proud of myself for that. Sandra starts walking towards me again, and I begin to back up when she launches herself at me. I hear the slap ring out before I feel the blooming heat across my cheek.

She's in my face now, rage shining in her eyes, "I told you to stop moving. Now, stop. Moving." She takes a step back but is still far too close for my comfort. Darting quick glances around the office, I look for anything close by I might be able to use and notice the phone is still lying on the desk.

God, I hope someone is still connected.

"Why? Why me? Why did you target me?"

"*Why?* Why?! What do you mean 'why'?! You stole him from me! We were going to come out publicly soon! That's why I took a job that was so below my capabilities! I was giving up my career to make him happy!"

I take a deep breath and try to rationalize with her, "Sandra, you guys were never together. He turned you down."

"Stop."

"You guys hadn't spoken in years—"

"Stop it!"

"Sandra, please just leave us alone. You're not even supposed to be here with the restraining order—"

"*I said stop it*! Stop talking!" She snaps and lunges at me with the knife, with a ragged scream pouring from her mouth. I try to move, but she manages to graze my arm, and the pain is sharp. I watch blood well to the surface and look up to see a scary, serene look come over Sandra's face.

Oh fuck.

Landon

I can hear voices in my office as I creep closer to the door.

"...don't worry. I'll make it quick! And Landon will be so happy with me for getting rid of you. You've become such a thorn in our side, always in the way. Always there. You're a distraction. You and that brat. Once you're gone, we can focus on us again."

Hope's voice is shaky when she replies, "He won't be happy with you. Besides, how could you be together if you're behind bars for the rest of your life?"

Sandra cackles, something that sounds completely unhinged, and I guess she is. "Don't you get it? Everyone thinks

I'm 'crazy'. No one will convict me. They'll feel sorry for me…"

I stop listening and turn to see my security team and the police come up behind me. Jamie comes to stand next to me before leaning close and whispering so as not to be overheard.

"Boss, I'm so sorry. With all the chaos, we didn't see her sneak in. Someone was down in the lobby screaming about a gas leak, and everyone panicked."

I can hardly hear him explain, I'm too focused on getting to Hope.

"Sir, don't. I can see the gears turning. I don't think barging in would be wise. The cops are here, let them do their job."

I turn, about to lay into him for standing in my way, when I hear a sharp cry of pain, and then I'm moving. There's no thought behind it, I just bust into the office. My eyes scan the space and I see them on the floor. I don't know or care how they ended up in the position they're in. All I see is Sandra on top of my baby girl with a knife, driving towards her chest. Hope is struggling to keep it at bay, and again, there's no thought. My legs are moving without my having to tell them to do so. I throw my weight against Sandra's side and send her flying off Hope.

In no time, I have the psychotic woman pinned to the ground with my cast across her throat and the hand holding the knife pinned by her head. The level of rage I feel seething through my body is something I've never experienced before. *Just a little more pressure on her throat and I could…*

"Landon." That's Jamie's voice. "Landon, you got her. She's down. Hope needs you, she's bleeding."

My head snaps to the side, and when my eyes land on Hope, I see her clutching her arm and a police officer kneeling next to her, examining the injury. I look back at Jamie, and he nods, removing the knife from Sandra's hand before taking my place and restraining her. Everything is a blur for the next few hours. Sandra is hauled off in cuffs, and I spend what feels like hours fielding questions from police, city officials, and employees. Hope and I are taken to the ER to be examined; her for any signs of concussion and to check that her arm doesn't need stitches, and me to check on my ribs and that I don't have any new injuries. Lizzie will be staying with her grandparents tonight to give us time to process what happened.

I pull Hope close to me while we lie in bed, and she burrows closer still, as if trying to bury herself under my skin.

"I'm so sorry, baby girl."

"You have nothing to apologize for. You didn't instigate or encourage anything with her."

I don't respond, because even though she's right, I still feel responsible. I should've reported her when she first came on to me. Maybe none of this would've happened.

Hope lays her hand on my face and gently turns my head to look at her, "Landon, look at me." I turn toward her, "I'm serious. Nothing you could've done would've made a difference. I don't think she's entirely stable, not with the way she was behaving. She seems to have fixated on you, and this would've happened with anyone she deemed a threat to her reality."

I sigh, "You're probably right, but that doesn't make me feel any less responsible."

"And that's okay, you're allowed to feel however you feel. Just don't let it consume you. We're both still here, together, and we will move forward as a family."

My chest expands at the sight of love and devotion pouring out of her eyes when she looks at me. Leaning forward, I give her a deep, searing kiss, which she returns enthusiastically.

It's only when we're both panting that I pull back, resting my forehead on hers, breathing in her scent, that I tell her, "I love you, baby girl."

She gives me a sweet smile, "I love you too, Daddy." Her lips turn into a flirtatious smirk when she adds, "Now fuck me."

EPILOGUE

THREE MONTHS LATER

Landon's recovery is finally coming to an end, and our wedding is coming up in two weeks. He wanted to wait until he was out of his cast so he could wear a suit, even though we're just having a backyard wedding.

Well, it'll be a backyard once the house is built.

It didn't take the police long to track down the hit-and-run driver. Sandra really doesn't handle rejection well. She has a history of stalking and assault and has been in and out of mental hospitals for years. Since they arrested her we've been assured that her behaviors are grounds for a more permanent stay in a facility where she can get the help she needs.

Reed Enterprises ended up buying the massive property the agency had been working on, and Landon immediately purchased it to build on for himself. Well, for *us*. He said we didn't have to sell the house Matt bought if I didn't want to, that we could rent it out when it came time to move, and that we don't have to move into the massive place they're planning until I'm ready, which was a huge relief. While I've made a lot of personal progress, I'm not quite ready for that. I think if Landon and I ever decide to have a kid of our own, that might be the best time to move. Until then, I'm happy where we are.

The last eight months have been an absolute whirlwind. I know some people think we're moving quickly, but our relationship has progressed so fluidly that it just feels right. Landon and Lizzie are damn-near inseparable. She's continued to call him daddy and when I see the warm look in his eyes every time she says it, I know I'm making the right decision in bringing him into our lives.

Landon has continued to help me with my own self-image issues. Since the accident, the mirror time-out has become a weekly ritual since his arm has been in a cast. I still hate it, but I will admit that my dislikes column has recently dropped a few things. I can actually look at myself in the mirror most days without wanting to look away. Even my friends and family have noticed a difference in the way I carry myself, how I walk with more confidence, with my head held higher. It's been so liberating being able to walk around proud of the things my body has done and to feel like I'm setting a better example for Lizzie.

As our wedding comes closer, my excitement only grows. I decided to get a simple white dress, nothing fancy by any means. I went online and searched "white dress" and scrolled through the options. I found one made of a gorgeous silk material. It's knee-length with thin straps and a sweetheart neckline. I wanted my "something old" to be the shoes I wore in my wedding to Matt, and when I asked Landon if he was okay with that he simply smiled, "I think that's a great idea. It'll be like he's there with us."

I have to say, most days I have a hard time believing he's actually cool with me holding on to parts of Matt. I never thought anyone would be so understanding of the memories and feelings I still hold for my late husband, but here we are! Landon surprises me every time he mentions and includes Matt in our daily lives. He still takes the time to talk to Lizzie about him, and now when she sees Matt's picture she points and says "daddy". The first time she did it, I was worried it would upset Landon, but all he did was pick her up with a soft smile, saying, "That's right, sweet girl! That's your daddy! Good job!"

Later that night, as I lay in bed with him I turned to him to tell him how much it meant to me that he's helping to keep Matt's memory alive. He pulled me close, "He's Lizzie's father and a part of you. How could I not? To disregard him would be disregarding pieces of the two girls I love most in this world. Besides, I'd like to think he would approve of me, that we'd be friends if he were here today."

"I think he would. I love you so much. Thank you for choosing us."

"I love you, too, baby girl. I can't wait to have you bound to me in every way." Looking down at my flat stomach, he reaches out to rest his hand over my empty womb. When he looks back up at my eyes, I swear his eyes are glowing when he says, "In *every* way."

Reaching down to cup him through his boxer-briefs, I give him my most salacious smile and suggest, "Why don't we start practicing?"

He doesn't even let me lean in to kiss him before he has me rolled on my back. He looks down at me with love, adoration, and promises of forever in his eyes.

We eventually fall asleep tangled in each other, sated and content. We have forever, and I couldn't be more thrilled about the years to come.

ACKNOWLEDGEMENTS

Wow. My first book is done and I couldn't be happier! I want to say a special thanks to my "Brain Trust" for helping me get this thing started, and for providing advice/information to help me further this story and make sure I'm not spewing a bunch of BS.

Thank you to my editors for making this novel readable and making me look literate instead of the idiot I'm sure I looked like prior to them getting their wonderful hands on it.

Thank you to my girl Caitlin for doing my cover. It looks amazing and I absolutely love it! I can't wait to see how books 2 and 3 come out!

Thank you to my wonderful contacts who helped me make sure my kinky shit was both kinky and true to reality! I would've had a hard time putting together the punishment scenes without you!

Thank you to my husband for supporting me and helping me make sure this book came out on time. I love you and appreciate everything you do for our family!

Thank you to Fable & Fern Literary Co. as well for selecting me as one of their first clients. Your help with marketing, social media, and ARC readers is utterly invaluable, I love you both!

BOOKS BY THIS AUTHOR

Bound To You

Series ongoing

STALK ME!

(but like, in a fun way)

Love this book? Tip &
message the author
with **Quilltips**!